# Just Living and Reproducing

## Victor Boc

# JUST LIVING
# AND
# REPRODUCING

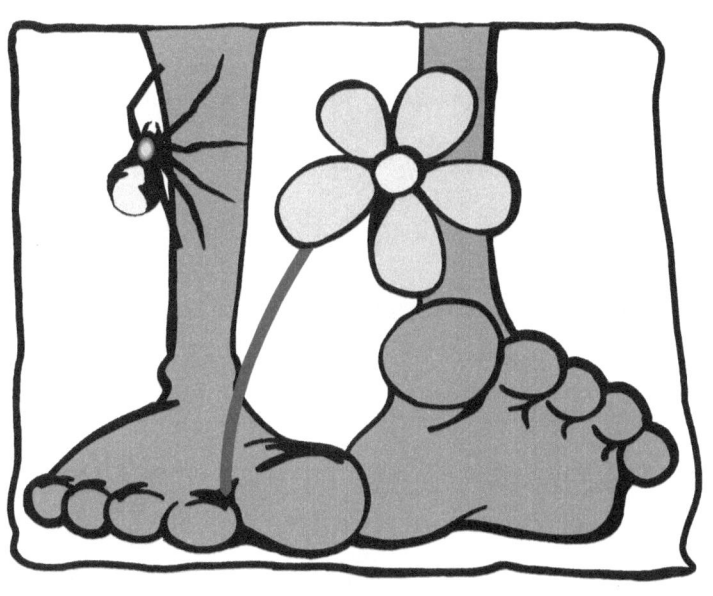

# VICTOR BOC

# VORCO PUBLISHING
## PORTLAND, OREGON
info@vorcopublishing.com

Portions Copyright © 1981, 1998, 2005 byVictor Boc.
First printing: Cody's Books, Berkeley, California.

ISBN: 978-0-912937-413-4
Library of Congress Catalog Card Number: 97-91144

---

Publisher's Cataloging in Publication — First Edition

Boc, Victor
    Just living and reproducing / Victor Boc. -- 1st ed.
    p. cm.
    Preassigned LCCN: 97-91144
    ISBN: 978-0-912937-41-0


    1. Short stories, American. 2. American poetry. I. Title.

PS3552.O3J87 1998                     818.54
                                      QBI97-41303

---

# JUST LIVING AND REPRODUCING
## — a collection of stories and such —
### Victor Boc

Kindle eBook: justlivingandreproducing.com/ab
justlivingandreproducing.com — vorcopublishing.com

Published in the United States of America.

This book is dedicated to
everyone I have ever known,
even Scott Kauffman.

*"Your book is really weird, Victor.
Maybe you should try writing about
herbs or health foods instead."*

— Dr. John Zaharie, Ph.D.

# CONTENTS

# Contents

# ALL MY EYES ARE FADING

Images once seen through dust
Now trust no more in my hope,
But grope for my glance.
The chance is gone.
I turn from the stage of thoughts
And see I'm the only one standing,
But handing my life to me.
I'll be less than what I've been.
The sin has been crushed
And will lie dead in the street
Till feet of ice can play its song.
No wrong, no right.
The bite of age is not seen,
For my keen vision is old.
The gold of life lies brown,
And I have no tears—only sound.
The next trip aims further into dust
And must be met with me
Eventually.
No deceit, no disguise.
For all my eyes are fading.

# FARMER JALION'S BARN

Duthton came home from school today and found a bug on his belly. It was a nasty looking bug, stuck tight, eating its way into his skin.

"Mommy," he screamed, "why do I have a bug stuck on my skin?"

"Because," she replied, "you are going insane. Whenever you find a bug eating its way into your tummy, it is a sure sign you are going crazy."

"But Mommy, is there anything I can do about it? Is there any way to stop it?"

With a stern face, Mommy looked down at her son. "You need to be a good little boy and always eat your spinach when you are told to."

Duthton knew this matter was serious.

The next day, he hurried down to the local produce market and bought a whole basket full of fresh spinach.

"Look, Mommy!" he exclaimed as he burst through the front door. "Look what I did."

"Wonderful, Duthton. You're such a good little boy," Mommy said, patting him on the head.

Without hesitation, she cooked up all that spinach right there on the spot.

Duthton, fork in hand, eager as can be, sat himself down at the table. Mommy brought out a huge heap of soggy spinach and placed it in front of him. With steady and sincere determination, Duthton gobbled up every last speck.

"Beautiful," Mommy declared when she saw his empty plate.

Then came the moment of truth.

Nervously, Duthton gripped the bottom of his shirt. Then, in one swift motion, he lifted it high, exposing his little white belly.

The bug was gone!

Duthton was so excited he ran around the house three times shouting obscenities.

"All right, all right, enough of celebration," Mommy finally said. "It is time now, Duthton, for you to go down to Farmer Jalion's barn, down at the end of the road, and stand on your head to make the pigs laugh."

Duthton did as he was told.

# DOORWAYS

Big golden doorways swing open and shut,
But not to enfold my love.
It's outside in the back yard
Spitting filthy grease balls at the sun.
Run to those weeping.
What else can I do? For me or for you.
See the pretty river flowing to its falls.
All the numbers change with time,
Even yours and even mine.
Some goal, some hope, some aim!
Name the train I'm riding,
Instead of always hiding.
A summer thought but empty,
A brilliant dream but dead,
Fed to time.

# MY FRIEND EARL

"Is that your spider?" I asked her.

"Of course, it's my spider," she replied, obviously pleased that I had asked. "He comes and sits by me every night."

She turned toward me. "And who is that you are oiling?"

"Oh, this? This is my friend, Earl." I was proud.

"And just what good is Earl to anybody?" she fired back.

"Well... he's a lot of good," I said, winding him up.

"Show me."

"Okay, I'll just plug in cartridge number 86, into the front here, and now you just watch."

"Hello, there," said Earl.

"Hello," she replied, not at all impressed.

"And what might *your* name be?" Earl was all smiles.

"It might be Jeannie," she said with a smirk.

"Might it? Ha, ha!" Earl performed an appropriate tilt of his head. "That's a lovely name."

Jeannie rolled her eyes.

"Pleased to meet you, Jeannie." Earl's voice was perfectly modulated. He allowed an adequate pause while gazing upon her in a gentlemanly manner. "Gee, you're looking good tonight, Jeannie. Absolutely ravishing. Can I get you anything?"

Jeannie glared at me.

"Would you like me to get anything for you?" he repeated.

"No." she replied, without expression.

"Oh, the pleasure's mine." Earl bowed slightly and continued. "Maybe you'd like something to drink?"

"I'm not thirsty."

"Okay, maybe later. You just holler if you want anything. Your wish is my command." Earl showed a toothy grin. "Do you come here often?"

"Not much."

"Oh, no? Are you from around here?"

"More or less." Jeannie rolled her eyes again.

"I see." Earl performed another timely pause. He then shifted his weight and wrinkled his brow to appear deep in thought. "Look, Jeannie, perhaps it's a little forward of me to ask this, but are you married?"

She obviously did not like the question. "No," she shouted, looking away from Earl and casting a side-glance at me.

"Gee, that's surprising," Earl said. "I mean, a nice girl like you not married. I am truly amazed. You know, Jeannie, I think you're a lot like me. We have a lot in common. I'm not married, either. I guess I never found the right woman."

"You don't say." Jeannie was clearly growing tired of the demonstration.

"But now you, Jeannie, I like you. I think you're a good woman." Earl stared straight at her. "Say, would you do me the honor of this dance?"

Jeannie glared at me. She was definitely annoyed.

"Jeannie," Earl continued. "May I request your company for this dance? It's a delightful melody, don't you agree?"

Her gaze intensified. Her eyes pleaded. I could see she'd had enough.

I reached over to Earl, threw the HOLD switch and pulled out the cartridge.

"Now, let's see what your spider can do!" I challenged. I was confident that Earl's performance could not be beaten.

"That's nothing," she said. "Just watch this."

The spider sat motionless on the table beside her. Slowly, she lowered her hand to the edge of the table. A moment later, the spider crawled across the table and onto her hand. It moved to the center of her hand and stopped.

Several seconds passed. Nothing happened. Neither Jeannie nor the spider moved.

A minute or so went by.

"What's he doing?" I blurted.

"Shhhhh!"

A few seconds later, the spider moved back across her fingers and onto the table. It returned to the same spot where it had been.

She extended her hand for me to see. And there... there, in the middle of her hand, was a tiny brown blob, a dab of goo about the size of a pinhead.

"Wow!" I exclaimed.

"Now that's natural!" she declared proudly.

"Wow!" I said again, truly impressed.

"So, how does that compare with Earl?" she asked tauntingly.

I was speechless.

"You see," she said, "Earl is no good at all. He's not the slightest bit natural. He's only a robot who knows only what he's been told. He can only do an appropriate action for any given situation. He has no ability to think things through for himself. He cannot be spontaneous. He only reacts, and only in the acceptable fashion. He has no beauty. He's nothing but a functional machine."

Her words were enlightening to me.

"Oh, he may fool some people," she continued. "His actions are proper enough all right. He's a good faker. But he doesn't fool me. Nope, I can tell. Your friend Earl is just no good to anyone at all."

There was no denying she was right.

"Don't you see? Earl is worthless. He's a disgrace, a total embarrassment. You should be ashamed to be seen with him."

I thought for a moment. Then I admitted, "I think you're right."

"Of course, I'm right!" she bellowed. "Earl is no good whatsoever. He might as well not even exist!"

With that, I plugged in cartridge number 22 and released the HOLD switch. Earl turned and faced me.

"Earl," I said softly, "listen, old buddy. We just realized something. Me and Jeannie here, well... we just figured out that you are not natural, Earl."

"What do you mean?" Earl asked.

"Well, I mean that you are nothing but a programmed machine. You do not actually think about anything. You're not capable of that. You can only react to circumstances in the appropriate way, the way you've been programmed."

"I don't get it." Earl appeared confused.

"The truth is, Earl, you're just not any good. You're not worth anything."

Earl stood quiet for a moment. "Am I too old?" he asked.

"No. No. It's got nothing to do with that. It's just that you're not natural, Earl. That's all. It's hard to explain."

"Is it that I'm too old fashioned?"

"No. Honestly, it's not that at all."

"Is it my appearance?"

"No. Nothing like that." I had to chuckle.

"I don't understand," Earl said helplessly.

"Hey," Jeannie butted in, "don't try to explain it to him. He can't grasp it. You're just wasting your time."

"Look, Earl," I said, "it really is hard to explain."

"I've always tried my best." A tear was forming in his eye.

"I know you have, Earl. And it's not that." I felt bad for my friend. "It's just that you're not natural, Earl. I don't know how else to say it. It's not your fault. It's nothing you can help, really."

"Would it help if I apologized?" Earl asked.

"No, Earl. You haven't done anything wrong. It's just the way you are."

Jeannie was becoming impatient.

"Okay, Earl, listen," I said. "I'm going to tell you this directly. The truth is that you don't deserve to exist."

"I just don't understand." Earl hung his head.

"I'm sorry, Earl, but that's just the way it is." I took a breath and continued. "This is it, Earl. We're going to have to turn you off for the last time."

"I guess I should say good-bye then," Earl whimpered, still looking down.

"Good-bye, and so long, old buddy."

Earl and I shared a firm handshake. Then I flipped off his main switch and removed the cartridge.

"Well...?" I said as I turned to Jeannie. She looked back at me and smiled.

With that, we both took a deep breath, as deep as we could, and held it. She nodded. Then, in unison, we both blew with all our might, directly at Earl. The force of our wind knocked him over.

He hit the ground with a tremendous crash.

Earl's body broke apart from the fall. His head split open, which exposed a dense mass of electronics inside his skull. It was packed solid with computer chips and wiring. Until that moment, I had not realized there was that much stuff inside him.

For quite some time, Jeannie and I stood there staring at the wreckage.

Then, I noticed something. Out of the midst of the electronics inside his head, something seemed to be moving. Squirming inside that circuitry appeared to be some sort of... what was it? Insects? Yes, some sort of insects were in there.

To get a better look, I walked over to his head. I glanced at Jeannie and she nodded approval. I reached down and pulled apart some of the wiring. And there, deep in the midst of all that electronics, was an entire nest of spiders. They had been in the middle of his head the whole time, just living and reproducing.

I came back to Jeannie, and we both stood there looking down. The spiders began escaping from their nest and spreading out over the ground in all directions. They left their eggs behind.

I looked at her, and she looked at me.

I felt sad for Earl, but I knew there was nothing I could do for him at that point. So, I reached my hand out for Jeannie. She took my hand in hers and we walked away together.

As we walked, we talked. We talked about our flower gardens.

# YOU AND I

Innocent gaze may be the way
With daylight shining on all our sins.
Away, a man sits squat in the dirt
And sells his time for diamonds and hurt.
And you and I back home in the grass
Throw love to one another
While the handfuls pass uncaught.
A fish swims by
In dry water raining.
Wonder what he's gaining dressed in frowns.
All the sounds you hear I fear.
We're near, but not together.
The kittens you're petting have eyes of sorrow.
Maybe tomorrow they'll kiss you,
Or maybe our song will miss you.
Am I wrong about the fish?
Inside our hearts, a dream has begun this day.
The sun plays with her too.
And you and I back home in the grass
May never know what to do.

# JEFFREY

Jeffrey was ten years old. Jeffrey was alone. Jeffrey was bored.

That gives you an accurate picture of Jeffrey at the start of our story. Imagine a little boy wandering around aimlessly day after day searching for something to do, and always lonely.

Our story begins one summer day, like most, when Jeffrey was trying to decide what to do for the day. His goal was to come up with something he could tolerate. Some days he would go to the park and sit on a bench. Other days he would walk down to the lake. Some days he would wander over to the bus station and watch the buses come and go. But this particular day seemed special somehow. He wanted something different.

Jeffrey decided he would go to the zoo. He hadn't been to the zoo in a long time, and he could always count on the zoo to fill the day with a unique kind of excitement. So, Jeffrey went to the zoo.

Most of the animals looked the same as the last time he was there. The giraffes were nice. The fish were nice. The tigers were nice. The hippos were nice. The seals were nice. The mice were fast for mice. The kangaroo was... hmm...

Jeffrey realized that he had never before paid much attention to the kangaroo. This time, however, he stopped to ponder the strange creature. How odd the animal appeared. Jeffrey felt sorry for the kangaroo. He felt sad that the animal was locked in its cage all alone. He couldn't help but wonder if the kangaroo was lonely, as he was. What does a kangaroo feel? he wondered.

Their eyes met. Jeffrey stared intently at the kangaroo. The kangaroo stared back.

And then, in an instant—it happened.

Jeffrey thought he heard the kangaroo say something to him.

But then Jeffery quickly realized that such a thing is impossible. Everybody knows that kangaroos don't talk. And Jeffrey knew, too.

So, he moved on.

Jeffrey spent a long time studying the bears—great big hairy ones. He looked at all the different types of birds—fat ones, skinny ones, birds with many bright and glorious colors. He saw all the different kinds of snakes, poisonous ones too. He saw camels, buffalos, elephants and all sorts of strange creatures. But you know what? The whole rest of the time Jeffrey was at the zoo, all he could think about, really, was his visit with the kangaroo. He could have sworn he heard that kangaroo say something to him.

At last, it was closing time. And Jeffrey went home.

That's not the end of our story, however. Nosiree. All evening, Jeffrey thought about the kangaroo. That kangaroo was the only thing on his mind. He knew the idea was ridiculous, but he felt certain the kangaroo had tried to communicate with him.

The next day, he was again haunted by thoughts of the kangaroo. Try as he may, he could not get that silly kangaroo out of his mind. He knew how dumb he was being to believe a kangaroo had spoken to him, but, thinking back, he was sure he had heard the animal say something. He tried desperately to cast the event from his mind, but he could not.

Days went by. But the passing of time made no difference. Jeffrey was unable to free himself from constant thoughts of the kangaroo.

Some days he'd be sitting at his desk in school, daydreaming out the window, when... "Jeffrey!" the teacher would suddenly shout. "What's the matter with you?"

"Oh, nothing," he'd reply nervously. But, of course, he was thinking about the kangaroo.

Then at home, at the dinner table, he'd be sitting motionless, staring at his plate, when... "Jeffrey, what's wrong?" his mother would ask. "You don't have an appetite today?"

Appetite or not, Jeffrey was lost in thoughts about the kangaroo. He knew there was no way a kangaroo could have spoken to him. He understood that logically. But no matter how he tried, he simply could not get the idea of that talking kangaroo out of his mind. Nothing worked to relieve his torment. The kangaroo was always there.

And things got worse. As time went by, Jeffrey became obsessed with thoughts of the kangaroo. Day and night, no matter where he was, no matter what he was doing, he lived with that kangaroo as his secret companion. The situation became unbearable.

Finally, he could endure the misery no longer. He knew what he had to do. He needed to go back to the zoo and see that kangaroo again. He was ashamed to admit the fact to himself, but he must go back.

Jeffrey realized that surely his obsession was stupid, but he had no choice: he had to give in. He yearned desperately to put his troubled mind at ease, and he certainly wasn't getting any relief by trying to forget about things. He simply had to return to the kangaroo. There was no other way to get beyond this problem.

The next day could not come soon enough. Right after breakfast, Jeffrey hurried to the zoo. Once inside the front gate, he ran straight for the kangaroo cage.

Jeffrey stood facing the cold, steel bars. Wide-eyed and willing, he peered into the cage at the kangaroo. The kangaroo looked back.

Silence. And then...

It happened! Jeffrey heard the kangaroo say something to him. No doubt about it, the animal spoke.

So, Jeffrey talked back. And the kangaroo talked again. And Jeffrey replied. And the kangaroo replied to that. They were talking! What a joyous moment!

Jeffrey knew the kangaroo could hear his thoughts, just as he could hear the kangaroo's thoughts. No words needed to be spoken. They were communicating better than had they been using words.

Jeffrey sat down in the dirt outside the cage. The kangaroo hopped over to the bars in front of Jeffrey and sat down inside the cage. Just like that, they stared at each other. No sound was made, but Jeffrey and the kangaroo were talking. They talked and talked and talked.

Hours passed. Eventually, the zoo closed for the day, and Jeffrey went home. And that is how Jeffrey came to know the kangaroo.

Every day thereafter, Jeffrey would go to the zoo and sit for hours talking with his new friend. He never missed a day; he went to the zoo every single day without fail. Some days he might not have as much time as other days, so his visit might need to be short. But he always managed to spend at least some time every day with the kangaroo. He was committed.

This went on for weeks. All the zookeepers came to know Jeffrey by name, and they expected his daily visits. They'd see him coming and call out cheerfully, "Hello, Jeffrey. How are you today?"

To them, Jeffrey was a nice but somewhat nutty kid who just happened to like staring at a kangaroo his entire life. They couldn't help but snicker among themselves when they saw the youngster sitting on the ground outside the kangaroo cage. The scene always looked the same: a little boy sitting outside the cage, a kangaroo sitting inside the cage, staring at each other through the bars, motionless for hours. It was a strange sight, to say the least.

And that's not all. Every day, Jeffrey would come home from the zoo and tell his mother about the talk he had with the kangaroo that day. According to Jeffrey, they talked about all sorts of things. They talked about their families. They talked about their different worlds. Mostly, they talked of faraway lands, of daring adventures, of hopes and dreams. They shared their every thought.

His mother, knowing this whole thing was a product of Jeffrey's imagination, felt she should humor him. She figured it was a phase he was going through and he would eventually outgrow it. She tried to understand, believing that whatever was happening must fulfill some sort of inner need Jeffrey had. Ever the optimist, she believed everything would be okay in the end. That theory would have been fine, except for the fact that things were about to get even weirder.

Jeffrey came home from the zoo one day and acted a bit more jittery than usual. Later that evening, he called his mother over to him and said, "Sit down a minute, Mom. I want to talk to you about something."

She sat down.

Jeffrey was obviously unsure how to proceed.

"What is it?" she asked. She was concerned.

"Well, I don't know quite how to say this, Mom. But the last week or so, I've noticed something, something really strange. I'm not sure what to make of it."

"What is it?" she asked again.

"Well, it's like this. The kangaroo is beginning to change..."

"Change?"

"Yeah. Change."

Jeffrey went on to explain that, day by day, the kangaroo was becoming more like a person, more humanoid. According to Jeffrey, the kangaroo's tail was getting shorter, its face was flattening and its thick grey skin was changing into flesh. Jeffrey spoke convincingly.

His mother did not know what to think. She had assumed that all this nonsense about the kangaroo would eventually pass. Now, she was not so sure. She knew children often have fantasies, but something about this one seemed outside the bounds of normal. She asked a few friends what they thought, but no one had any ideas. Most people suggested she just give the matter a bit more time. So, that is what she did.

As weeks passed, Jeffrey spent more and more time at the zoo. And he became increasingly more firm about his claims of the kangaroo changing. Instead of tapering off, Jeffrey's relationship with the kangaroo became even more intense.

Months passed.

Every day, Jeffrey would spend all his spare time at the zoo. And every day, Jeffrey would come home to his mother and report the daily changes in the kangaroo. According to Jeffrey, the animal was looking almost human now.

It had been many months since Jeffrey first talked with the kangaroo, and in all that time, he had never missed one single daily visit. Clearly, the situation was not getting better. His mother was now seriously considering the possibility of getting professional help for him, but she continued to put it off, hoping and praying that the problem would improve.

Another month passed.

And every day, Jeffrey would go to the zoo. Nothing else interested him. He spent every minute he could sitting outside the kangaroo cage. That was his life.

Then, one day, the impossible happened.

The day began like any other. Jeffrey was down at the zoo, sitting in the dirt outside the kangaroo cage. When, suddenly... he noticed!

The change was complete!

The animal inside the cage was no longer a kangaroo! It was a human being in every way! Jeffrey leaped to his feet and gave a joyful yell.

He raced over to the nearest zookeeper and insisted that the man come with him. The zookeeper, of course, knowing Jeffrey, was reluctant to go. He couldn't help but chuckle. But Jeffrey, pulling with all his might, dragged the man by the arm all the way over to the kangaroo cage.

When they got there, Jeffrey pointed inside the cage. In a firm little-boy voice, he declared, "Look there, mister zookeeper. That's no longer a kangaroo you have inside this cage. It's a human being!"

The zookeeper peered into the cage. He stopped chuckling. His mouth fell open. "Yeah, you're right!" he said. "Doggone, kid, if you ain't right!"

With that, the zookeeper unlocked the cage. And the two friends walked away together, arm in arm.

# COOL

I've tried to be cool
And keep my journeys to myself.
I've cried when I should cry.
I've built doghouses for all the neighbors' dogs.
And still...
The guilt I've killed won't die!
The beds are filled with lovers.
The kings hate the mud.
Mud's good when a bee stings.
I'm free of things that drool.
Too bad no one could know me
And see that I've been cool.

# CRUETS FOR A BUTTERFLY

## 2013:

I have long been wondering what is going on. Since I was a child, I have sought answers. What is the secret of the universe? Why are we here? What is really happening beneath the illusory world we see? All my life, I have been searching for truth, somewhere.

Today, I went back in the woods and sat by a place I know. A spring of fresh water flows there. I sat for a long time, pondering the nature of reality. Hours later, I realized that I had become no wiser as a result of my pondering. I laughed at myself. How silly I am.

Then I got a crazy idea. Just for fun, I knelt down at the edge of the spring. I thrust my hands into the water and began throwing handfuls of it high over my head. For no particular reason, I shouted, "I declare this the Spring of Wisdom. Henceforth, all who shall drink of its waters shall know true wisdom and bliss."

I lowered my head to the water and drank. I laid back and gazed at the sky. And waited.

Nothing happened. I felt no surge of knowledge, no special bliss. What a wacky thing to do.

I left the woods laughing. It's fun to play.

## 2113:

You know how butterflies flutter, don't you? As it happened, this particular butterfly was fluttering aimlessly through the woods. From fern to fern it would bounce, without apparent purpose. At last, deep in the thick of the forest, it came to rest on a marble stone.

The stone was a historical marker, placed next to a little spring. On the stone was inscribed:

*THE SPRING OF WISDOM*
*Consecrated on the 13th day of March, 2013*
*by Sylvester Hanscranch*
*who, on that day, thrust his hands into the water*
*and proclaimed:*
*"I declare this the Spring of Wisdom.*
*Henceforth, all who shall drink of its waters*
*shall know true wisdom and bliss."*
*May ye drink of her waters and bathe in happiness.*

On the marble monument the butterfly sat, soaking up the afternoon sun. Its yellow wings and red and black markings appeared bright and spectacular. High above, the sun's rays poured through the trees and made their way straight into the little pool of water.

A short time later, there came unto this peaceful place a short, chubby man. He waddled along, carrying two empty water pitchers under his arm. Immediately, he spotted the gorgeous winged creature and said, "Hello, pretty yellow butterfly. How are you today?"

The man stopped directly in front of the marble stone. He put his hands together and bowed reverently. Then he continued speaking.

"You know, pretty yellow butterfly, you would do well to worship this precious spring of water here. There is no limit to the secrets it can tell. It is as if God Himself bathed in her waters so many years ago."

The man gazed deeply into the water.

"Perhaps, He is still amidst her waters, I do not know. Many strange and miraculous truths have been revealed to me right here, pretty yellow butterfly. I have experienced revelations that neither you nor I could dare question, nor fully understand."

The man knelt next to the water's edge.

"Here, let me help you, pretty yellow butterfly."

With that, the man bent over and dipped one of his pitchers into the water. "Here is the water of truth and cleanliness," he announced, raising the pitcher to the sun. "May it cleanse your soul and allow the pure light of happiness to shine through."

He set the pitcher of water on the marble stone next to the butterfly. The butterfly flapped its wings a few times but did not fly away.

"Take ye and drink of this water," the man offered.

The butterfly flapped its wings a few more times and then stopped. It remained motionless.

The man stared at the butterfly for several moments. A frown gradually came over his face. "Perhaps you think you are too good for this water," he said with a touch of anger.

He bend down and filled the second pitcher.

"Well, then, take ye and drink of this, for this is wine. With this vessel, I give you deep red wine, suitable for the table of God Himself. This is wine transformed from the water of the Spring of Wisdom."

He set the second pitcher next to the first on the marble stone.

The man stood still, staring at the butterfly for a long time. In his eyes, a look of aggravation was building, as if he were witness to a grave sacrilege: the butterfly blatantly defying the forces of heaven.

The man kept staring, frozen by his anger.

Suddenly, the butterfly flapped its wings and rose into the air. It bounced up and down, around and around, fluttering about randomly. Eventually, it drifted away from the scene and disappeared into the forest.

# SITTIN' ON A LOG

I'm just sittin' on a log,
Got my head in a knot.
Ought to know what to do,
But I'm 'fraid that I'm not.
Many years to begin with,
Many more to be told.
How old must I get before I'm not old?
Sally walks up beside me.
She sits down to think.
Her mind glows of story.
Her breast glows of drink.
There's love to be had here.
There's peace to be earned.
How smart must I get before it's all learned?
This log is not our homeland.
Our bed is not our sins.
We might as well be downtown,
Selling time for grins.
It means something somewhere.
It's plain to see, I'll bet.
How much must it rain before I get wet?

Please sit tall my darlin'
And know life is good.
My soul's outside singin'
Flyin' high like it should.
I'm ready for our union,
Which you'll give to me.
How much must I show before I can see?
I'm just sittin' on a log,
Got your rain check in my hand.
Think someday I'll be happy,
Someday I'll understand.
Then we'll be the moon,
And we'll be the sun.
How much must I do before I am done?

# DINNER AT THE McGUIRE'S

The dinner began like any other dinner at the McGuire household. Mr. and Mrs. McGuire and their young son, Adam, sat at the table eating their meat and potatoes.

The silence was broken when Mrs. McGuire spoke. "Adam," she said, "would you please touch that chair next to you?"

Adam looked up from his meal. His face turned from blank to confused. "What?" he asked.

She repeated the question. "Would you please touch that chair next to you?"

"Why?" Adam asked.

"Because I'm afraid it will jump up and bite me," his mother explained. "But it won't jump up and bite me if you'll just touch it with your finger."

Adam set his fork down and sat up straight. He glanced at his father. Mr. McGuire was concentrating on food, apparently figuring that the conversation would take care of itself without his help.

"But, Mommy," Adam said, facing his mother, "a chair can't jump up and bite you."

Mrs. McGuire was not happy with her son's response. "But I believe it can, Adam. I'm getting scared." She looked her son in the eyes. "I'm your mother, Adam. Please do it for me now."

"But it's not true, Mommy. A chair can't bite anyone. It's not possible."

"Please do it, Adam." His mother was becoming impatient. "Can't you see I'm scared? If you care about me, then please do what I ask. Help me!"

Adam thought for a few seconds. Then, he leaned forward and spoke in a deliberate manner. "But, Mommy, your belief is wrong. I think the best way for me to help someone with a false belief is to let them see the truth. The best thing for me to do is to *not* touch the chair, and let you see that it won't jump up and bite you. Don't you agree?"

Mrs. McGuire lowered her eyes to the plate in front of her. When she looked up, tears were forming. "So, you just don't care, is that it?" She started whimpering.

"Oh, no, Mommy. That's not true. I do care about you. Very much. Don't you see that by allowing you to experience the truth, I'm doing the best thing for you that I could possibly do?"

"It sounds like some sort of an excuse to me," she offered.

Adam took a deep breath and let the air out slowly. "No, Mommy. I love you."

A tear broke loose and started to roll down Mrs. McGuire's cheek. Realizing that her son was not complying with her wishes, she began to squirm and fidget. She turned her head quickly from side to side as if searching for something to look at. Adam watched, hopeful she would somehow find solace in his words. She did not. At last she could contain herself no longer.

"For God sakes, Adam!" she burst out. "Why are you making me so miserable? Why do you have to behave like this?"

The increase in volume caught Mr. McGuire's attention. He was suddenly interested in the conversation. He put down his napkin and looked across the table.

Adam brushed back his hair and straightened his glasses. He did not like seeing his mother upset, and he certainly did not want his father getting involved in this. He cleared his throat. He looked straight at his mother and proceeded to talk calmly.

"Mommy," he explained, "please try to understand that the source of your discomfort is your paranoia about something that is not real. Believe me, I am not trying to make you upset. But I really want you to see that there is no danger here for you. You are just making yourself upset for no reason."

"Why are you doing this, Adam? Why are you torturing me?" she yelled.

Adam could feel his father's eyes upon him. He knew the situation had better cool down right away or things could turn ugly.

"I firmly believe that the truth is always best, Mommy." Adam went on to explain, "When you see that the chair will not bite you, then you will be rid of this silly fear forever. The truth will set you free, Mommy."

Mrs. McGuire began to cry out loud.

"I admit," Adam continued, "that it would be easier right now for me to give in and touch the chair for you rather than try to explain this, but in the long run..."

"Please, please, please!" Mrs. McGuire shouted. "Just touch the chair for me, please! What's so difficult about that? Oh God..." Mrs. McGuire was trembling. She had entered a state of panic. She looked as if she were trying to grab onto something but couldn't because her hands had nowhere to go.

"But, Mommy..."

Mr. McGuire leaped to his feet. "God damn you, Adam!" he shouted. "You won't even help your own mother!"

Adam stiffened. He knew trouble had found him. He turned to face his father, while of course, trying to avoid eye contact.

"I don't know where we went wrong with you, kid," his father yelled. "It's pretty sad when you won't even do something for own your mother, the person who brought you into this world. What's wrong with you?"

Adam dared not reply. Mr. McGuire looked down at the table and slowly moved his hand back and forth across the surface while formulating what to say next. Adam waited patiently. Then the man looked at his son and commanded, "Now get the hell up to your room. I don't want you having any fun for a week, do you hear? Get out of here. Go!"

Adam stepped back from the table. He stopped and looked at his mother. She peeked up at him, biting her lip as tears rolled down her cheeks. Her eyes seemed larger than usual.

Adam knew he shouldn't speak, but he gave it one last try anyway. "But..."

"And don't you dare talk back to me, young man!" his father blared. "Now go! Or I'll hit you so damn hard you'll never know what hit you! I've had all I can take from you. Now get the hell out of my sight!"

Adam turned to leave.

"You'd better shape up fast, kid, or life's gonna be pretty rough for you," his father added.

Adam left. His footsteps could be heard as he made his way up the stairs to his room. Gently, the door shut behind him.

Mrs. McGuire looked horrible. She sat in her chair quivering, terrified, her face dotted with tears. Her makeup had run.

Mr. McGuire turned to his wife and smiled, a smile in which she found comfort. As he stepped toward the chair in question, his wife watched his moves with great interest. Slowly and deliberately, Mr. McGuire laid his finger on the chair.

With that, Mrs. McGuire let out an immense sigh of relief. She sunk back in her chair and, with the sleeve of her blouse, wiped the tears from her face. Safe and secure once again, she let her arms fall limp to her side. With eyes of gratitude, she looked up at her husband.

He was smiling at her.

She smiled back.

# WILLIE

Willie was sittin' by the seashore. What for? I don't know. But anyway, he was just sittin' there gettin' bored.

So, Willie decided to go into the water. But he did not to go into the water as you or I might go into the water. Not at all. Willie was more clever than that.

Willie began to shrink. He got smaller and smaller. Then, when he thought he couldn't get any smaller, he got smaller still. Then, he went into the water.

Willie sat down on some scum. How come? I don't know. But anyway, he was just sittin' out there no bigger than a flea, sittin' there on a thin layer of scum floatin' on the water. Willie was just sittin' there takin' in the big bright beautiful sunlight. Yeah, it was nifty!

He was havin' a blast. It was a lot of fun for Willie, checkin' out the scum and everything. He must have been there like that for a long time.

But after a while, he got bored again.

So, Willie started shrinkin' some more. This time, he got really, really small. He kept shrinkin' like there was no tomorrow. He got so small that he could see the minuscule particles of scum. But that wasn't small enough for Willie, so he shrunk some more. He got so tiny that he could actually crawl into the molecules that made up the particles of scum. Whoa! That is small! That's what he did, he crawled into one of those molecules.

There he was, just sittin' there on one of the atoms with his feet danglin' over the edge. That's where he sat. Why's that? I don't know. But anyway, he dug this scene a whole lot, bein' on an atom and all. The whole thing was real interesting to him.

But, eventually, he got bored again.

This time, Willie decided he would just keep gettin' smaller and smaller until he found someplace where he would never get bored. He sure did start shrinkin'.

Willie got so small that the atom seemed huge to him. There was so much empty space inside the atom that he didn't know where to go. He headed toward one of the electrons. He kept getting smaller and smaller. The electron was actually kind of illusive, bein' real fast and uncertain all the time. But as he kept shrinkin', he could see that the electron was made up of a whole bunch of very tiny... somethings. Better keep getting smaller, he thought.

He got so small that these tiny somethings seemed very far apart. They were weird sort of things, kind of glowing and hot looking. He picked one in particular to explore. All the while, Willie kept gettin' smaller.

Willie noticed that the something was actually a tiny ball of yellowish fire, or at least it looked like fire. When he got small enough, he noticed that this bundle of fire had a number of miniature balls rotating around it. Willie was intrigued. He enjoyed exploring new places.

Willie decided to pick one of these itsy-bitsy revolving balls and study it more closely. He got smaller. And then smaller still.

At last, he was small enough to come down and land on one particular ball. It was solid. In fact, he got his feet wet. The ball had some areas of land and some areas of water. How 'bout that! Willie had landed right by the edge of where the land met the water. He looked around. He was flabbergasted!

Willie sat down.

Willie was sittin' by the seashore. What for? I don't know.

# YOUNG AGAIN

A miner in the hills
fills his wagon with coal,
while his golden dragon
is stolen from him.
Foolish sage!
In a rage, he kisses you.
Kathryn the poet knits in her cubby,
while her hubby sits on the pot.
It's hot this month in Niles.
She smiles a lot while her children dress,
and the Evening Press sets on the table,
unable to be read.
Asleep in her bed, she kisses you.
The slaves and beggars meet at dawn.
They gather to issue demands.
With lawsuit in hand, their spokesman appears.
The crowd cheers him on.
They know what they want, with nearly no doubt.
They shout and shout and shout.
But none of it matters—
When their time runs out, they kiss you.

I blew out the candles.
My wish will come true.
You'll come to my house in town
and glow with newness and good,
like Humpty Dumpty once could.
I'll run to greet you, my guest,
and I'll feel my best when at last we meet.
Gently, I will kiss you.
Gently, young again.

# THOUGHTS OF A WEST COAST BEE

Hi there, human. Mind if I talk to you a minute?

I'm sorry I can't stop. I'll need to keep working while I talk. You don't mind, do you?

You see, this time of afternoon is the busiest time. I have to find as much pollen as I can, or else I won't be doing my part for our hive. So, don't mind me if I seem busy. That's how bees are, you know.

It sure is a gorgeous day today, isn't it? Look at those tall trees over there shining green in the sunlight. Isn't that a wonderful view? The sunlight makes the clover look better, too. Even the grass looks divine today. Don't you agree?

I wonder, how does everything look to you today, human? Does the sunshine make you happy, too? What sort of thoughts are going through your mind as you sit there in the grass?

Hey, I just thought of something. I'll bet I look the same to you as all the other bees around here. Do I? Well, you know what? You look the same to me as all the other humans. How about that? But don't take it personally, okay? I mean no offense.

Hey, how about that bee over there? Huh? Does she look the same to you as all the other bees? Ha-ha, probably so. But not to me. No way! She's gorgeous. And she's found a nice full bed of clover, too. Yeah, now that's a beautiful sight.

Hmm. But you know what? You know what I can't help but think, human? I can't help but think that she's only alive at this point in time. I mean, so what! I mean, to you she looks the same as all other bees, right? And next year, she'll be dead and I'll be dead, and there will be some other bees out here in the same place doing the same things. And the whole thing will look the same to you, and yet it will all be different. Or will it, really? What do you think about that, human?

Do you ever think about that sort of thing when you see another human? Do you think that you're only alive for a short period of time? True, humans live longer than bees, but it's still just an instant really.

Someday there will be other humans out here to replace you and all your friends, and they'll do all the same things you do. Do you realize that fact, human, when you look into the face of another human sparkling in the sunshine? And when another human's body calls to you with love, do you think of that? Do you realize you're only alive now, and that's all.

You know something else, human? Even if you had not come here today, I would still be sitting on this same clover flower right now going about my day's business. That's a frightening thought, you know. Think about it. Even if you had not come out here this afternoon, even if you were in some other land, even if you were east of the great desert, I would still be here right now doing what

I'm doing. And the sun would be shining just as brightly on all us bees, and the same breeze would be blowing across the grass—even if you had not found your way to this particular clover bed where you happened to plop yourself today.

In fact, most of the time, you humans don't even notice us bees, do you? You really should pay more attention.

Do you want to know how we feel about you, dear human? Okay. The truth is, we don't need you, or any of your kind. And don't you think for a minute that we do. I don't mean this to sound snotty or anything, but we bees were doing this sort of thing long before you humans started poking around these parts. Don't think that just because you happen to stumble over here one fine day, that I need your presence to think these thoughts. Not at all. Even when you don't hear my thoughts, I am still thinking them.

I don't want you getting a false sense of your own importance here, human. This area is our stomping ground, not yours.

Come to think of it, I don't believe I've ever seen you here before. Where've you been, human? Huh?

Obviously, we bees don't need you. In fact, right now, at this very moment, far away from here, in some clover patch where you may have once happened to sit long ago, some other bees are busily scurrying about. And the scene there looks just like the scene here. After all, when you come right down to it, bees are bees.

You know, we have bees all over this country of yours. Wherever you go—East Coast, West Coast or anywhere in between—there we are. Except in the desert. There's none of us in the deepest part of the desert. Once a bee is on one side of the desert, the bee never gets across. It's not possible. The bee will live and die on the same side. Did you ever think about that?

Oh well.

Anyway, I need to get going now. I have to go do a dance back at the hive. I need to let the other bees know about this place. There's a whole lot of pollen here, more than I can gather up myself. We have more than thirty thousand workers back at the hive, and I sure could use some help.

Did you know that as a team we brought in more than forty pounds of pollen and nearly sixty pounds of nectar already this summer? How about that? We figure we've made almost four million trips averaging about five miles each, just in the past three months. Pretty impressive, huh? One thing about us bees, we are good workers. And we get a lot done, too. So, that's why I have to go do a little dance right now. It's all part of my job, you see.

It's too bad you can't come along to watch my dance. I think you'd find it pretty amazing. My dance will tell the others exactly how far and in what direction they should go to find this patch of clover. I wonder, could you do something like that? I'd like to see you try to communicate that information as effectively as I do. Heck, we bees do it better than you humans ever could, even with all your fancy words and mobile technology and the like.

So, I guess I'd better get going while there's still some sunlight left. It was nice talking to you, human. It's probably best if I shut up now anyway. Really, I shouldn't be telling you my thoughts in the first place.

Besides, I'm not supposed to know all that stuff I told you. I'm only supposed to know the clover beds in this area and how to communicate that information to other bees at our hive, and that's all. I'm not supposed to know all those facts and figures about geography and other things. And I'm not supposed to know where this area is relative to the mountains and the desert and the coast and all that.

I'm not even supposed to know I'm a West Coast bee. That's your job to hand out the names.

So, I'll just shut up and go.

See ya.

# SLOW

I can see it now.
She's slow.
Oh, to be slow!
In days of old.
In days of lace and frills
    and old glory,
When the church was white
    and children ran out front in the yard,
When a gentle breeze blew
    and an old brown cap
        hung on a post on the porch.
She's slow.
She needs slow.
She needs what once was
    and is no more.
She needs what was real
    when time was never heeded.
She's here but really there,
    where time was slow
    and love was true.

# HUBERT

Everyone liked Hubert. He was a leader and an innovator. His fellow employees at the Brenton City Utility Plant remarked often about his dynamic personality. Even the supervisors considered him an outstanding individual. Hubert was admired by all who knew him.

One lovely evening in June, Hubert was attending a party. Whenever there was a party, Hubert was there. This particular party did not appear different from any other party that Hubert normally attended. All the usual faces of the Brenton City popular crowd were there. And everyone was behaving exactly as would be expected.

About midnight, the party began to drag. Most people had gone home, leaving about a dozen folks scattered around the room, each acting as if the party were still bustling. Maybe none of them noticed that most of the guests had left; maybe none of them were sober; maybe none of them cared what was happening outside their own thoughts. In any event, those who remained were nervously trying to act pleased with the situation.

Each person had two reasons for still being there—one was the reason he wanted everyone (including himself) to believe was the reason he was there, and the other was the real reason. For example, Mary wanted everyone to believe she was there because she was totally engrossed in talking to Emily about the color combination of the dress that Sandy wore to last Friday's luncheon. Mary was talking loudly. Mary was, in fact, there because Larry was there, and she adored Larry. Larry, meanwhile, was busy telling Walter how good the local football team will be this fall. Walter was trying to act interested in what Larry was saying, but he was secretly wishing he could just listen to the CD that was playing at that moment. Bill, on the other had, was sitting in the corner alone. He was trying to act as though he were engrossed in the music, while he was really longing for Emily's attention. The CD was almost finished playing anyway.

Amidst this scene, Hubert spoke up. "I have an idea," he announced.

"What is it?" asked Margaret.

Margaret was pretty much associated with Hubert, or so it seemed. You know how slow these things can be sometimes.

"I know a place," Hubert explained. "It's down by a stream, back in the woods. It's a quiet little place where I go sometimes by myself. There's a nice spot to sit on a rock by the bank and watch a little waterfall. It's really a beautiful place at night. We could all go there now. We can walk there from here."

Everyone agreed. Well, almost everyone: Bill didn't say anything but he quietly slipped out the door and presumably went home. And Jason and Roberta disappeared as well. But all the others acted as though they were eager to set out on the adventure.

Their enthusiasm did not last long.

The group headed out the back door of the house and across a vacant field until they came to the edge of the forest. There, they stopped.

"The place is about a quarter mile back into the woods," Hubert announced.

From where they stood the woods looked dark and ominous. Several of the group wanted to return to the house. So they did. Only Hubert, Margaret, Tom, Sherry and Walter decided to go on. Those who went back did not allow themselves to feel regret, however, since they agreed that the novelty of the idea had already worn off.

The five courageous souls gave themselves a pep talk and ventured into the woods.

The journey was slow and arduous. They had only one flashlight. Stumbling over sticks and rocks, they made their way carefully. They kept going. After twenty minutes or so, they arrived at their destination.

Indeed, the place was beautiful. Each one took a turn shining the flashlight around the area, expressing how natural and unspoiled the surroundings appeared to be. They decided to settle in and stay a while. They all quickly took on the appearance of totally at ease.

Walter situated himself the furthest downstream. He sat on a large rock, acting as though he wasn't the least bit concerned about being alone. Tom and Sherry settled about twenty feet away from Walter, closer to the waterfall. They sat on the ground together and, for the moment, were talking about Mrs. Fenderson's new car. Tom probably wanted to hold Sherry's hand, but didn't. Sherry may have wanted to hold Tom's hand, too, but you would never know it. About twenty feet away from them, Hubert stood next to Margaret. They were holding hands.

Hubert shined the light directly across the stream from where they stood. Some ivy hung down to the water from a cliff above. Hubert demonstrated how his voice echoed when he shouted in that direction. "Hooooo! Hoooooo!"

That presented an ideal opportunity for Margaret to display her adventurous spirit. It was also an ideal opportunity for her to demonstrate her independence and how she did not allow holding Hubert's hand to limit her freedom. Margaret let go of Hubert's hand and removed her shoes. Then, as Hubert aimed the light for her, she waded across the shallow stream to the other side where the ivy hung. As she splashed her way across, she turned around and shouted that she wanted to discover the source of the echo. When she got to the other side of the stream, she pulled the ivy aside, revealing a tunnel.

"Look!" she exclaimed.

Even Walter looked up.

"Let's see where this tunnel goes," she yelled to the others.

Tom, Sherry and Walter said the water was too cold and, besides, they were comfortable right where they were. They promised to stay there and wait until Hubert and Margaret came back.

Hubert took off his shoes, waded across and joined Margaret on the other side. Then, the two of them slowly waded into the tunnel. The ivy fell back into place behind them.

Judging from its appearance on the outside, you would have expected the tunnel to be small and cramped. But such was not the case. Once inside, there was a feeling of great spaciousness.

Hubert shined the light around. It was an immense tunnel, with plenty of room to stand upright. The tunnel appeared to be at least ten feet wide. Both sides and the bottom were solid concrete. About six inches of standing water covered their feet. It was very dark, so dark that without the flashlight, their exploration would have been impossible. It smelled somewhat musty.

Slowly and carefully, the two made their way through the tunnel. Although they did not need to hold hands for safety reasons, they held hands anyway.

The tunnel kept going. It was much deeper than they originally expected.

They had walked about fifty feet or so when Hubert discovered something. Against the left side of the tunnel, he saw some steps built into the concrete wall. They were strong metal steps that protruded about six inches from the wall. Obviously, those steps were put there to allow someone to climb up the side of the tunnel. Hubert and Margaret stopped to study the steps. Both of them were puzzled. Where could anyone possibly climb to in a tunnel? they wondered.

Hubert shined the flashlight up, but the light did not illuminate anything. Only darkness.

"Where did the ceiling go?" Hubert asked out loud.

"I don't know," Margaret replied.

"This doesn't make any sense," Hubert said. He was intrigued.

"It's creepy," Margaret offered.

And it was.

"Well, these steps must go somewhere," Hubert declared. "What do you say we climb them and see where they go?"

"Oh... I don't know about that." Margaret shook her head. She was adventurous all right, but there were limits. "Why don't you go up a little ways, and I'll wait here."

"Are you sure?"

"I guess so."

"You're scared, aren't you?"

"Well... kind of."

"Tell you what," Hubert suggested, "I'll leave the flashlight with you so you'll be less frightened. You wait here. I'll just be a few steps up the side of this wall. I mean, how far could these steps go, really?"

"Okay. I'll be all right. You go ahead."

"Are you sure."

"Yeah. Just be careful."

It was decided.

Hubert took the first two steps very slowly and carefully. He stopped and looked down. Margaret was shining the flashlight up in his direction, but clearly the batteries had become weak. Then he took two more steps, also slowly. Then a few more steps. Then, he picked up the pace. The metal steps did not hurt his bare feet as he had suspected they might.

He kept climbing.

When he first started climbing, Hubert felt certain that he would be back down with Margaret after only few seconds. I mean, how far could the steps go? He figured that, surely, he couldn't possibly climb more than ten feet or so before the steps would have to come to an end.

But he was wrong. The steps didn't end.

Hubert kept climbing.

And then climbed some more.

Hubert climbed and climbed.

It was dark. Hubert could not see anything, let alone determine where he was going or what his surroundings looked like. But he was not about to quit. He kept climbing. And climbing. And climbing.

And climbing.

He lost track of time, but surely he'd been climbing for fifteen minutes or so. He stopped to rest. He was tired. And he was dumbfounded!

Hubert couldn't believe what was happening. It made no sense. Where was he going? How could he climb so high when he was in a tunnel deep in the woods? What was it that the steps were built onto? Where the heck was he? Hubert was confused. If only there were some light, he thought. If there were light, he could see what was going on. How could this be? None of this made any sense.

At that point, Hubert was faced with a decision. Should he go back down the steps or should he climb onward? It was not a easy decision. He'd been away from Margaret for quite some time now, and she was undoubtedly worried or freaked out down there. He yelled for her. No reply. And no light from the flashlight. What happened to her? he wondered. Was she still down there waiting?

On top of that, Hubert was terribly tired. He was exhausted. He surely did not feel like going further. On the other hand, he didn't want to give up, either, because... well, the reason had something do with finishing what you start. Hubert pondered his dilemma.

He looked up again. He squinted and looked carefully into the distance. Then he saw it.

Hubert spotted something he hadn't noticed before. He detected a tiny dot of light, high above. It appeared to be very far away, but yes, it was definitely a speck of light.

That did it. That made his decision for him. Hubert decided to go onward. He resumed climbing.

Time passed. But Hubert had committed himself to climbing to the end, so time no longer concerned him.

He climbed and climbed and climbed.

More time passed.

After climbing for what seemed like an hour, the tiny dot of light was only slightly larger. Apparently, it was very far away, indeed. But Hubert was not deterred. He felt tired and sore, but he refused to quit climbing. He was determined to reach the end of the steps.

As he climbed, he allowed his thoughts to wander. He made no attempt to control the stream of ideas entering his mind. He thought about whatever came his way.

Hubert kept climbing—and thinking. He thought of his childhood. He thought of his mother. He thought of his schooling. He thought of what he had done with his life, of what he had become. He thought of his joys and his sorrows, his likes and his dislikes. He thought of his purpose in life, whatever that might be.

There was time for thinking. He did not need to pretend or put on any sort of act. After all, he was alone. Dreadfully alone.

At one point, Hubert hummed a song. It was a melody his mother had sung to him when he was a child. The sound soothed him.

All the while, he climbed. And climbed.

Hubert had always enjoyed his own company, but for some reason, while climbing those stairs alone in the dark, he felt as if he were meeting himself for the first time—as if he had been lost and now was found. In a sense, he was discovering who he was. Something as important as that must surely take a lot of time, he figured. But time was something he had.

Hours passed.

The source of the light didn't become discernible until he had been climbing for what must have been three hours. It was incredible, the time it took to complete this climb.

Hubert could finally see that the dot of light was actually a round opening of some sort. And he could tell that every step he took brought him closer to that opening. He was exhausted, but he climbed anyway.

At long last, he arrived.

He had reached an opening about three feet in diameter. Cautiously, he pulled himself up and through.

He emerged as though climbing out of a manhole onto the ground above. Slowly, he planted his feet and stood up straight. He took a deep breath. The air was fresh.

Hubert's mouth fell open in amazement. He stood in the middle of a vast field of grass—beautiful, bright green grass as far as his eyes could see in all directions. The sun was shining brightly. And although the sky was clear, the smell of a fresh rain filled the air.

The land was flat. There were no trees, just grassland shining in the sun. All directions looked the same.

Hubert decided he did not want to climb back down that hole. It was too dark. It was too damp. It was too...

Hubert put his hands into his pockets and began to walk. It didn't matter which directly, so he just walked.

In no time, he had wondered off into the distance, far away from the hole from which he had emerged.

And he never went back.

# DAWN, DUCKS AND BOLD

It sure is hot.
It's not like I thought it would be.
"Three days and three nights is all it will take."
That's what they tried to tell me.
Now I'm without food or water or breeze.
No trees are in sight.
I might never get out of this desert.
Then...
In the distance, I see you coming,
Drumming on a box you have in your hand.
You cross the sand and come toward me.
For once, I don't feel the heat.
We meet.
"My lover," you say, "I have brought you gifts."
You throw open the box.
I eat the food.
I drink the water
And pour it all over my head.
Refreshed and content, I reach out to thank you.
But you close the box
And continue across the sand.
The land soon swallows you up.

I remember you.
And I believe...
Through it all, your eyes look back
To the ducks in the pond
And through the sun to the worlds beyond,
And you say very softly beneath your breath,
"I know, my son, I know."

# THE LADY

Mommy and her little girl were taking a stroll down Main street.

"Mommy," the girl questioned in innocent wonder, "is that a lady over there?"

"No," Mommy assured her. "That's nothing more than a female with high-hat and dress—at best, perhaps a woman."

Mommy pointed down the road. "Now, over there, Silvie, there's a lady. She sits all alone in her garden with shovel and pail—not frail and not stale. Only the pure of heart would dare try to touch her. To love her, love must rule. Her clothes are simple; her beauty springs from within. It may seem sly or it may seem shady, but there really is no faking in the making of a lady."

Across the street, Leroy the Lover was instructing his younger brother, Samuel.

"Look over there, Sammy." Leroy pointed. "You see that chick walkin' down the street with high-hat and dress?"

"Sure do."

"Well, Sammy, I'm gonna get that woman into bed with me. Here's your first lesson in how to get chicks to put out, Sammy. All you gotta do is fill 'em with lies and push 'em around a little. It works every time."

Samuel looked around. "What about that woman in that garden down the road?" he asked. "She looks nice."

"Naw," Leroy said, "She ain't my type. She looks too cold. We wouldn't hit it off, me and her. Now, this chick here, man, I could do her. Yeah! She's for me."

Samuel realized that there really is no faking in the making of a lady.

# LIFE IN JOKEVILLE

I am a little raindrop
Falling to the Earth.
I know not where I come from.
I know not of my birth.
Soon I'll fall and hit the sand.
The land will swallow me up.
I'll dissolve and fade away.
Where do you suppose I'll be then?

There is a tiny schoolhouse hidden away in the land of Jokeville. It's an eight o'clock class, and the students are tired. And bored. They sit in a gray room—gray walls, gray ceiling and gray blackboard. Up front, the teacher paces and babbles. He's skinny and bald. He's wearing a grey suit. Nobody knows what he's talking about, not even those who are awake.

Sandy sits in the back row. A fly crawls across her desk in front of her. She swats it with her math book, and it's squashed. The whole class turns to see what happened.

Mrs. Jones just gave birth to a baby girl. It's a beautiful, healthy baby. Little known to anyone, the child will grow up happy. She'll become a secretary at the Jokeville

Mining Company, where she'll work until she gets married. She'll have three wonderful children and love them all equally.

She'll love the rain, too.

# JOGO

Jogo go
Make your way in the caves
Go now boy
No time to play
Hurry to your duties
Scurry day by day
Go Jogo go
Show us all the way

# HEAD

Head was a head. He knew what he was: he was a head. And that was that.

He had two eyes, a nose, a mouth, a couple of ears and everything a head should have. His skull was big toward the top, and his forehead was high. He figured a high forehead probably meant he had a lot of brains. And that was good.

He was bald, but he had a thin covering of fuzz above his ears that he considered hair. His eyes were strong, set deep in his skull. Head felt he could win a staring contest with the best of them. Although his vision wasn't the best, he thought maybe he had some special power of perception with those eyes of his.

His nose was small. His lips were thin and delicate, as were his ears.

Head knew he had a neck, but he wasn't sure just how far down it went. Perhaps it went down four or five inches. Maybe it went down to some shoulders or something like that. He wasn't sure, but he knew there was at least some neck there. He was sure of that, and that was good. What difference does a boundary make anyway? He knew what he was—he was a head.

As always, Head was alone.

And then, Head heard a voice. He had never heard a voice before. At least now he knew his ears were working, to some degree anyway.

"Capastics."

Head did not reply. Then he heard it again.

"Capastics."

Head knew what the word meant.

Capastics were lip covers. They were made of thin metal, and they fit over your lips. They came in pairs, one for the top lip and one for the bottom lip. They were supposedly easy to put on, and they fit snugly. Their purpose was to protect your lips.

But Head didn't want them. He had decided long ago that he would hate wearing them—and his opinion was the only opinion there was. He knew he was right.

Again he heard the voice.

"Capastics."

This time the voice sounded closer, somehow more present. Still, he did not answer.

"Try a pair of capastics." The voice was loud and clear.

"No," Head replied.

"Try them."

"No," he repeated.

There was a moment of silence. Head could hardly believe he was carrying on a conversation. Actually, he was thrilled to be conversing, although he didn't like the subject matter.

"They'll protect your lips," the voice continued.

"I don't like them," Head replied.

"Have you ever worn them?"

"No."

"So, how do you know you don't like them?"

The voice made a good point, but Head knew what he knew.

"I just know I don't like them." Head spoke firmly.

"Oh, come on. They're natural. It's expected that you wear them."

"I won't like them," Head asserted. "They'll feel cold on my lips."

Head had always been comfortable. That's one thing he could say; he'd always been free of irritating discomfort. He valued his comfort, and he hated the thought of risking his comfort for anything. Besides, he knew he was right. He had his views and, come hell or high water, he was going to stand up for what he believed. He was a head of principle.

"You're just being bullheaded." The voice continued. "Come on, Head. Don't waste time. Put on a pair of capastics. You have to."

"No, I don't have to," Head declared.

"Yes, you do."

"No, I don't. Don't tell me what I have to do!" Head was now at a point of irritation.

"I'm sorry, Head. But you have to. It's a necessary step along the way toward getting the shield."

Head knew what the shield was. The shield was the final step. Once you put on the shield, it was all over. Then you were finished putting things on. But you couldn't put the shield on until you had everything else on first.

Head had seen pictures. The shield was made of some sort of transparent plastic. It fit over your entire skull, leaving only your facial area exposed. It consisted of two halves, hinged at the top. Both halves were shaped to fit tightly over the sides of your head and then fastened together under your chin. Once the shield was in place, all of your head was covered and protected.

Head didn't even like hearing the word. Just the mention of the shield increased his resolve.

"Listen, I don't want to wear capastics or the shield."

"You must."

"No."

"Yes."

"No!"

Silence. But head knew the moment of quiet did not mean he had won the argument. The voice was simply preparing its next point of attack.

Then, in a soft and persuasive tone, the voice spoke again. "Look, Head, let me explain this to you calmly. Capastics do not, in any way, hurt you. They protect you. There is no harm to you, only good. I understand your reservation, but you do not see the situation clearly. With all due respect, I must tell you that your concerns are unfounded. It is silly of you to object to something that is good for you. Don't you see? So, come on now, won't you try a pair of capastics? At least give them a try. Won't you?"

Head did not want to reevaluate his viewpoint. He could not allow himself to do so. He had to stand firm. He knew he was right. He didn't know why, and he couldn't argue against the logic expressed by the voice, but he knew he had to maintain his position. He didn't have time to worry about details of logic anyway. The bottom line was that he did not want to try them on, and that was that. Even if there were good reasons to do it, there was still the fact that he didn't want to. And that was enough.

"No," Head responded, a bit belatedly.

"Yes. You will."

"No, I won't"

"Yes."

"No."

"Yes."

"No, no, no!"

This time, the silence lasted a long time. It seemed like days, or at least hours. Head was beginning to think he'd heard the last of the voice. Then it returned.

"Head, let's be reasonable." The voice was almost soothing, obviously wanting to start over on a good note. "How about a moustache?"

"What?" Head was genuinely surprised at the change in approach.

"Would you try a moustache? It's really very simple. You just clip it on. It only takes a second."

But time was not the issue here. This was a matter of principle. "No. I don't want to. Please, just go away," Head pleaded.

"Why won't you at least give it a try?" the voice persisted.

"The hairs will scratch my skin."

"No, really. It doesn't bother you at all. It feels good. You'll like it. You'll be glad to wear it. It won't affect you in the slightest. You'll see."

"I don't want to," Head said firmly.

"Come on, let's not go through this again. Try it on."

"No."

"You must."

"No!" Head shouted. "I want to be free! I don't want anything touching me. Don't you get it? I want my skin

74

to be free and fresh. I don't want things around. I want nothing but to be free. Free! Geez, can't you take a hint? Go away!"

"You're wrong. You are being stupid again!" The voice was louder now.

"I am right, and you know it," Head declared.

"No, you're not."

"Yes, I am."

"Try on the moustache. You must sooner or later. Why not now?"

"No."

"It's a necessary step to the shield."

"I don't want the shield."

"Of course, you do."

"No, I don't. What do you know, anyway? Take your dumb shield and get out of here."

"You must wear it. It's normal."

"Never."

"You will. You'll see."

"Maybe you think so, but I won't."

"Yes, you will."

"No. I won't."

"Yes, you will."

"No, I won't!"

"Yes, you will."

Head was tired of arguing. He let his turn to reply pass. But the break in dialogue was brief. A few moments later, the voice was back at it again.

"Head, dear friend, listen to me. There is no need for all this hassling. Let's not argue. Let's not keep shouting at each other. What do you say?"

Head did not answer.

"Maybe we should go back to the capastics then. What do you think?"

Head remained quiet.

"Yeah, let's go with the capastics. Let's not worry about the moustache for now. Just put that out of your mind. Let's do capastics. How about it?"

Still no reply.

"Maybe now that you've had a chance to think about it, you're willing to give capastics a try. Would you do that? Come on, you'll like them. Why waste time resisting any longer? Let's give them a whirl, okay?"

Head shook his head.

"Capastics?"

"No!" Head shouted at full volume. "No!"

"Do it. Wear them. You must. Do it."

"For the last time, I do not want to wear any of your junk. No! Now go away!" Head was screaming loudly.

"Try them."

"No! No!"

Again there was silence. Head could not remember ever wishing he had legs, until now. If he had legs, he could run away. He knew the silence would not last long, and he was right.

"How are your eyes?"

One thing about the voice, it was persistent.

"How are your eyes?"

Head did not answer. His vision had always been poor, and he knew it.

"Hey, I asked you a question, Head. How are your eyes?"

Head hated the question. His eyes were a touchy subject.

"You're eyes are bad, aren't they?"

Head remained silent.

"Head, how are your eyes?"

"Yes. My eyes are bad," Head admitted.

"Your eyes can be good with glasses. If you wear glasses, you will see better. Wouldn't you like that? Wouldn't that be great? To finally see well? To see all you've been missing all these years?"

"No."

"You're eyes are bad, right? Your vision stinks, am I right?"

Head did not speak.

"Then don't be silly. Glasses will help you see better. They're a good thing, not a bad thing. You will like them. If you—"

"I don't want them!"

"But why not? You're being silly."

"Because I just don't, that's all. The frames will be cold against my skin. They'll be cold on my nose and along the side of my face."

"That's not true, Head. They warm up in a matter of seconds. Your skin will warm them quickly. And then you'll be able to see perfectly—forever. Believe me, it's well worth it. Doesn't that make sense?"

Head was silent. And tired.

"Be reasonable, Head. Act in your best interest. Wear glasses."

"No, I don't want to."

"Now, don't start arguing again. Don't be ridiculous. You must wear glasses. You really do want to, you know. You're just afraid to come off your position. But that doesn't matter. Just do the right thing. Try them."

Head wanted to counter with some awesome argument, but he had none. He had no refutation for the logic he was hearing. "No," was all he could muster. And it was a weak 'no' at that.

"Come on. You know you really want to."

"No. I... I..." Head could feel his resistance slipping. He didn't like the feeling. But he was tired of arguing.

"Wear them."

"But..."

"Wear them."

Head wanted this to end.

"Wear them. Don't worry about backing off your stand. Everyone changes their mind once in a while. It's a sign of inner strength to change one's mind. Come on, let's give glasses a try."

Head tried to show no hint of expression, but he knew he was not succeeding.

"Head? Are you ready to improve your life?"

Head did not move, except for a tiny bit of quivering he could feel in his lower lip.

"Head, I'm waiting. I've got your glasses right here. All you need to do is try them on. Perfect vision awaits you. It's all good, Head."

"But..."

"Come on, put them on right now. Let's get this over with."

"I..."

"Wear them."

"But..."

"Here you go. Wear them."

Head was so tired.

"Wear them."

"I really would rather not."

"Don't be stupid. Wear them."

"I..."

"You'll be glad you did. I promise."

"I..."

"Wear them."

He just couldn't take it any more.

"Wear them."

"Okay, I will."

Head didn't think of it as giving in. He thought of it as being reasonable. He figured that he was intelligent enough to weigh the pros and cons and see if glasses might be a good thing. After all, he had lots of brains, right? So, he was doing the wise thing by giving glasses a try. No big deal.

But just glasses! Nothing more!

The glasses were cold. But the voice was right; they did warm up in just a few seconds. And he could see better. Much better. Head looked around. Wow, everything looked so clear and sharp.

Head was wearing glasses. He didn't know what to think about that, but everything seemed to be all right. For now.

"How are they?" the voice asked.

"All right."

"Good. Then now you'll try capastics."

Head could not believe his ears. What's with this voice, anyway?

"Are you ready to try capastics?" the voice asked.

"No, I'm not. Don't you ever back off? Now, go away. Let me have some peace, please!"

The voice carried on. "I told you the truth about glasses, didn't I? I told you the cold would not bother you, and it doesn't, right? I told you that you'd be able to see better, and you can, right? So, would I mislead you about capastics?"

Head was silent.

"No, of course, I wouldn't. Capastics protect your lips. That's all they do. And they feel even more natural than glasses. And I'll bet you're glad you tried on the glasses, aren't you?"

Head wasn't sure about that. True, he could see better, but he still disliked the idea of something being on his face. And he could feel them. Even if they weren't cold, they were still there.

"Sure, you're glad." The voice answered its own question. "So, why not try capastics, too. You'll be glad you did."

"No," Head stated. "And that's final."

The voice started laughing. "Final? Give me a break! Don't be ridiculous. Of course, you'll wear them, just like you did glasses. Stop being such an idiot."

Head decided that the voice was not nice. He didn't like the voice.

"You think you got your opinions," the voice went on. "You think you're so high and mighty with all your viewpoints. Well, I'll tell you something, your ideas are wrong. Your opinions are crazy and unfounded. The sooner you give them up, the better off you'll be. But you're too ignorant to see that. So, you cling blindly to your beliefs, even though you know they are wrong. I just disproved them to you by showing you the benefits of glasses. You sure are one pigheaded son-of-a-gun."

Head just listened. He knew he was losing his resolve, and he didn't know what to do about it. The voice was wearing him down.

"You're really not stupid, Head. Why are you acting like you are?"

"I don't want—"

"Try the capastics. You must."

"No."

"I won't go away, Head. As long as it takes, I'll be here. I will never leave until you try them. This will go on forever! How's that sound? You want that?"

Head had no reply.

"Did the glasses hurt you?"

"I suppose not. Not really."

"Then what's the problem? Capastics won't hurt you either. Try them on."

"But..."

"Geez, you're difficult. Do it!"

"But..."

"Wear them, Head. Now!"

Head was so very tired.

"Wear them!"

"But..."

The capastics were cold. They were just as cold as the glasses were. But they, too, warmed up quickly. Unlike the glasses, however, they were extremely bothersome. No way could they be called comfortable. Head could not ignore the fact that he was wearing them. They pinched and poked in a weird sort of way. As soon as he put them on, he was overcome with a sinking feeling that perhaps he had made a mistake.

"How do they feel?" the voice asked.

"I don't like them," Head replied.

"I understand," the voice continued. "Sometimes they are a bit uncomfortable at first. You gotta get used to them for a little while."

"I thought you said they'd be comfortable."

"Well, they can be a tiny bit unfamiliar, but only at first. That's why you need the moustache."

"What?"

"The moustache."

"No way!" Head was outraged. He couldn't believe what he was hearing.

"Oh, come on. You know you're going to object for a while and then give in. Come on. Wear the moustache."

"I tried your glasses and your lip covers, isn't that good enough? Now please just leave me alone. Please!"

"I'm afraid I can't do that, Head."

"Please, please. Why won't you just go away?"

"I'm here for your own good. I am dedicated to you."

Head felt like crying.

"Wearing the moustache tends to soothe the irritation from the capastics," the voice explained. "You need them both together to get the full effect. It's actually a bad idea to have one without the other."

"Now you tell me!"

"Here is the moustache. Now, put it on."

Head was becoming less sure his objections even mattered. What difference does it make? he wondered. Maybe if he tried the moustache, he could get that horrible voice to shut up. One thing for sure, he was definitely not resisting very effectively. In fact, he had already failed. Twice! And he didn't even know if that mattered!

"Another reason you should wear the moustache is because it protects the area between your nose and your capastics. Doesn't that sound good?"

Quite honestly, nothing sounded good to Head.

"You know you will wear the moustache eventually, so why waste time? Put it on now."

Head figured he should object to someone telling him what he thinks. Maybe some other time he would have objected, but right now, he was so very, very tired.

"Wear it, wear it," the voice hounded.

"Will it scratch?" Head asked.

"No."


But it did scratch. The moustache bothered him more than the capastics. Head was now a bundle of discontent. He felt miserable—and confused.

"Earrings," the voice demanded.

Head would have objected, but he knew resisting was futile. He didn't have the strength. Anyway, how much could wearing one more thing hurt?

But when Head heard the word "Shield," that was a different matter. That was the final straw.

Head took inventory of himself. There he was, wearing capastics, moustache, glasses and earrings. And he was totally uncomfortable. He wondered how he had let this happen. He regretted ever conversing with that miserable voice in the first place. Head was thoroughly disgusted with himself. And the fact that he was now ready for the shield reawakened his fighting spirit. The realization that the shield was next gave him new cause to stand firm and fight. Why, he wondered, had he ever agreed to wear anything at all? What was he thinking?

"Shield," the voice repeated.

"Absolutely not. Now get out of here!" Head insisted.

"It's the final step. And then I'll go."

"I refuse."

"You refuse? Man, are you stupid!"

"I can refuse if I want to. I want my skin to be free!"

"You want your skin to be free?" The voice started laughing. It was a loud and obnoxious laugh. "You want your skin to be free, do you? Look at yourself! It's a little late for that now, don't you think? He wants his skin to be free! That's a good one!" The voice laughed and laughed.

"I say no shield. No. Now stop pestering me," Head declared in his assertive voice.

"You're a moron!"

"Leave me alone. I have my principles and that's that."

The voice busted up laughing again. "Your principles? You got no principles! You got nothing, you clown! Look at yourself! You're wearing glasses, moustache, earrings, capastics... You resigned your principles a long time ago. And now you want to make noise about some idiotic principles you never had in the first place? Give it a break!"

Head could not escape the feeling that the voice was right. Like it or not...

"Look," the voice continued, a bit more nicely, "you're almost there. You've already given in on your principles, so there's no point in pretending they matter any more. You've got one final step. It's not going to make any difference now."

"But I don't want to."

"I know you don't. I understand. But look at it this way. Even if you don't ever put the shield on, you will still be wearing the earrings and the capastics and the moustache and the glasses. You'll still be wearing all that. You will still have given in. Am I right?"

"I guess so."

"So, you might as well go all the way. I'll tell you—and I mean this—that's the only way you'll ever get rid of me now. And you want to get rid of me, don't you?"

"You're right about that!"

"No matter what happens now, you will have no principles. You've already sacrificed those. Nothing can change that now. If you refuse the shield, you'll just be a halfway sort of head. You'll be a laughing stock. You won't be worth anything at all. Do you want that?"

"I don't know any more." Head was so incredibly tired of this discussion.

"You know, the only way now is to complete what you started. For crying out loud, wear the shield."

Head realized that the voice was right, again. For the first time, he began to entertain the thought that maybe he had been wrong the whole time. Maybe everything he thought and believed in the past was, in fact, incorrect.

But no! He would not admit to being wrong! He could not! No! Never! In one last-ditch burst of rebellion, Head decided to fight on. He must not give in.

"No," Head shouted. "My skin wants to be free."

"What a joke!" the voice replied.

"My skin needs air!"

"Your skin will rot!"

"No. I will not wear the shield."

"The shield will protect your skin. You will be safe. The shield is good for you. Why do you resist what is in your own best interest? Wear it. You must."

"No."

"You know you will. No matter how much you resist right now, you know, sooner or later, the shield will be upon you."

"No, never."

"Your skin will not be safe unless you wear the shield. Your precious skin will rot without the shield."

"My skin will be free."

"You skin is not free now! It will never be free again. And without the shield, it will rot away."

"My skin will be free."

"It will rot."

"I will be happy."

"You will be miserable. You'll still be wearing all the items you're wearing right now. Without the shield, you'll be incomplete, unhappy, meaningless. You'll be confused. Your skin will rot. The shield will protect your skin and complete you. The shield will release you from your misery and allow you to be happy."

Head did not speak.

"You are such a fool not to see that the shield is what you've been longing for all your life. It is the source of joy for which you yearn. And you, fool that you are, resist it. Accept it! Celebrate your good fortune! Wear the wonderful shield! It is the only way now that you will ever find peace and happiness."

Head was so tired. So very, very tired.

"The shield is the most natural thing in the world. And you are so lucky. You are ready for it. You are fortunate, and you don't even know it. Wear the shield."

Head let loose a deep yawn. And the yawn hurt.

"Wear the shield."

The voice was right. There was no way out.

"Wear the shield."

Head felt ashamed. He was not the head he used to be.

"Wear the shield"

Head shuttered at the thought.

"Wear the shield."

"And you'll leave me alone?" Head asked.

"Yes."

"You promise?"

"I promise."

The shield took a long time to put on, and it didn't seem to fit right. Head inquired several times whether the shield was the right size for him, but the voice was no longer there to reply. The shield took what seemed like forever to warm up. In fact, parts of it never did warm up fully. The truth is, the shield was extremely uncomfortable. Head was more miserable than he ever thought possible.

But at least the voice was gone.

Once again, Head was alone. In the quiet, he could get in touch with his true feelings. He had time now to put everything in perspective.

He told himself that nothing important had changed, that everything was as it should be. He told himself that life was grand.

And it was.

After all, he could take comfort in the fact that he was still a head.

Yes, Head was a head.

And that was that.

87

# THE CHARGER WITH A HUMP

Seven dogs
Lost one and then there were six pigs
Six pigs
Lost one and then there were five herons
Five herons
Lost one and then there were four moolahs
Four moolahs
Lost one and then there were three clouds
Three clouds
Lost one and then there were nine geese
Nine geese
Lost one and then there were five blues
Five blues
Lost five and then there were flowers
A flower
Which we found
So that made a total of eight
Eight rivers
Lost four which was the one we found
A charger
A hump

And more...
I'm sorry the story's all a mess,
A less than elegant tale.
But there's one thing I see that's clear:
I'm here.

# THE LAST IDIOT OF CONNIEYL

I'm starting to drift away now. I guess I really want to get back to my lady who recently turned into a horse.

It's my own fault, though, you know. I had hold of one end of the rope, and someone in the truck had hold of the other end. I didn't know who it was. I swear, I didn't. I still don't. But whoever it was, they were seated on the passenger side. That much I can tell you.

I didn't know who the driver was, either.

The truck was a small pickup truck. The rope was slack, and the truck was speeding past me. I knew the slack would be taken up when the truck went by. That much I knew.

In a moment's impulse, I wrapped my feet around the fence on which I was sitting. I confess. I did it.

The truck raced by, and, sure enough, the rope snapped tight. Out of the truck window, holding the other end of the rope, came a little horse, flying through the air. She was such a tiny creature. She shot out like a bullet and landed awkward on the ground. She was injured. That much I could see.

I ran over and buried my head in her mane.

"I didn't know it was you, honest!" I pleaded. But it was too late for apologies. That much was certain.

Later, I took the horse home and laid her on the couch in my living room. She just kept getting sicker and sicker. I called the doctor, but he never showed up. It's been hours now, so I don't expect he ever will.

She doesn't groan too much, but I can tell she's getting sicker by the way she keeps squirming and wildly kicking her hoofs in the air. She's acting really crazy. Who knows what evil oddities she may have in her system by now.

You can see why I want to get back to her, can't you? You can see why I'm so desperate to reunite with her. You can see how much I long for her.

I do love her. That much is true.


Mona, where are you? Why don't you come to my view and exist? Why don't you? Please! Baby, baby, Mona. Oh, my Mona.

Say, would you like a sweet treat? Or a gum-purple smile?

Do you hear me, Mona? How far away are you? Where will you be this time tomorrow? Where are you now? Are you coming to our world? Tell me, Mona! Tell me!

How are you tonight? Do you exist beneath the same skies I see? Do you think with my patterns? With our thoughts? Or do you not exist at all? Tell me, Mona. Can you tell me?

Why don't you come? Whoever you are—why don't you show?

Where are you now, Mona? Do you know?


And now, nothing remains of the fishermen who came to shore this afternoon. Beneath my watchful eye, they scurried. The heroes told their tales and left the docks undisturbed. Maybe tomorrow I'll have fish for dinner. That's about all.

Tell me, my scholars, where did it take place that I turned my lady into a horse? I remember it so well, like it was only today. I loved her. Am I an idiot?

All you kings, queens, dukes, clerks, bankers, businessmen, bums, pigs, dogs, lovers, Christians, Buddhas and rivers, tell me. Do you have the slightest clue?

Where is she now? Tell me how to find her. Point in which direction I should go. Hills? Valley? Desert? Or must I lie here in agony alone?

Have you ever seen a flower shine?

Please, be all right, young princess. I will return someday. Please don't continue without me. Or without me is the whole thing meaningless?

How long ago did we walk together? Does the ocean remember? Was everything somewhere else then? Or is that idea meaningless?

I wish I knew. But I will wait. And I will wait with new dreams to tide me over. And new heroes to ward off the fear.

New lives. And new stories.

All built on old ground.

Good night, my sweet Mona, good night.

# MY OFFERING

Take my hand
      Take my glove
Take my heart
      Take my love
Take all that I am
      Take all that I was
Take for good reason
      Take just because
Take for your mother
      Take for your son
Take some for Jesus
      Take some for fun
No one will see you
      No one will care
Take more than you need
      Please don't be fair
All life is public
      Puke, blood and spit
The world is in torment
      My soul doesn't fit

You do me a service
      You do a great deed
Take joy in my stabbing
      And watch my gut bleed
Take all of my losses
      Take all of my gains
Then come back tomorrow
      And take what remains

# BAPTISM IN REVERSE

The outdoors was a bore, so I came inside. I thought I'd hide my insanity. Reverend Jones was the man to see.

I had no appointment, so I had to wait.

His lobby was plain and simple as a lobby should be, just right for the man, the mother, the kid and me. The man was not with the mother, but the kid was with the mother, who was reading *Christian Life* as best she could.

We sat there for hours, just staring and caring about the future of the wallpaper pattern.

Just when the music was improving, the man stood up. All our eyes were upon him (even the nun who had joined us and never stopped muttering to herself about her rosary beads or some such thing). The man slowly walked over to a tray of flowers in the corner of the room. He stood there a few moments looking down at them. Then, he lifted the flower tray off the stand, turned, and walked across the room in my direction. He stopped directly in front of me and, without uttering a word, dumped the entire tray of flowers over my head, dirt and all. Then, he walked back across the room, set the empty tray back on the stand and sat down.

At that moment, another nun entered the room and immediately glared at me. Her eyes seemed to ask why it was that I sat there with dirt and flowers all over me without even a watering can.

Before I could reply, the nun who was seated with us stood up and grunted. The two nuns embraced, said a few kind words to each other and then promptly hurried through a side door, a door marked "Shadow Room." I couldn't help but wonder what anyone would use a Shadow Room for.

I have to tell you, this was no thrill for me. There I sat with dirt and flowers all over me, trying to decide what would be an appropriate course of action.

I looked at the kid, who looked back at me in apparent disgust. Then, suddenly, the child got up, tromped across the room and stood before me. What now? I wondered. Without warning, the boy vomited in my lap. And he was a loud vomiter.

The mother quickly ran over to her son, gave him a slap, told him he shouldn't do that, pulled him back to his chair and handed him a copy of *Mental Health Digest*, which he then digested.

Just then, one of the nuns charged back into lobby from the Shadow Room. She had a worried look on her face. She gazed long and hard at me. I don't think she ever blinked. I knew she was wondering about the vomit. But she never mentioned it.

I found my situation unpleasant.

"Hey," I shouted, to no one in particular, "how long must I sit here like this before someone will bring me something so I can clean up this mess?"

Reverend Jones apparently heard my shout. He came running into the lobby and stood before me.

He smelled like incense.

I tensed. I could sense his disapproval.

He looked down at me and, with a soft voice, barely audible, said, "You should be ashamed of yourself."

I couldn't take any more.

So I got up and left.

Come to think of it, I really had no good reason to see the Reverend anyway.

# INTERVIEW WITH BUB

"Hello, and welcome to *Speak Your Mind*. My name is Richard Walker. With me here today is Bub. He's just a regular guy. Welcome to the show, Bub."

"A pleasure to be here."

"So, what's it like being a regular guy?"

"Oh, it's pretty ordinary, I guess."

"Have you always been a regular guy?"

"As far as I know."

"What about your parents? Are they regular people?"

"Well, my mother's deceased. I guess that's pretty regular. My farther sells shoes. Is that regular?"

"Well, yes. I'd say so."

"Well, then yes, my parents are regular people."

"What about you, Bub? Where do you work?"

"Wait, let me say something. I don't think you can tell if someone is regular just by where they work."

"That's true. You have a point there. So, what is it, Bub, that makes you such a regular guy?"

"I assume you're not referring to my bowel movements, right?"

"Ha-ha! No. I'm not. Good one, Bub."

"Well, I'm not really sure. I remember one night at Joe's Pool Hall with a couple of buddies. This was a few years back. And Chuck, he was one of my buddies, he turned to me and said, 'You know, Bub, you're just a regular guy.' And ever since then, I just knew I was."

"Do you like being a regular guy?"

"It's okay."

"But what do you think it is, Bub—what one quality determines if someone is a regular guy?"

"I'd have to give that some thought."

"Well, think about it. What is it?"

"I suppose it's that they are well adjusted, that they fit into society good and are comfortable with the world around them. You know, that they're normal."

"Now wait a minute, Bub. Nobody likes to admit they are normal. I mean, you go to any household, any walk of life, and talk to anyone, and they'll say how weird they are. They'll say how their life and their friends are so weird. Everyone thinks of themselves as different from the norm, don't you agree?"

"Yeah, you're probably right."

"I mean, if we had to rely on people saying they are normal, there wouldn't be very many normal people around, even those who really are. But now you, Bub, you're not ashamed to say you're normal, am I right? Do you think you're a normal person?"

"Well, when you put it that way..."

"For example, what sort of food do you eat?"

"Food?"

"Yes, what do you like to eat?

"Oh, just regular stuff. What everyone else eats, I guess."

"What sort of movies do you like?"

"Action movies."

"Who did you vote for in the last election?"

"I didn't vote."

"What's your religion?"

"Just regular Christian, I guess."

"All right. Let me ask you this, Bub. This might sound a little off the wall, but maybe this will tell us something. What sort of dreams do you have? I mean, when you're sleeping, what do you dream?"

"Wow. Strange you should ask that question."

"Why's that?"

"Well, I was just thinking... Sometimes I get this feeling that I'm dreaming when I'm awake. You know, that all of this is really a dream. And I was just having that feeling when you asked me that! Wow, that's freaky."

"I'm not sure I understand, Bub. What do you mean?"

"Well, like sometimes I feel that all this is unreal. I feel a bit light-headed or something. It's kind of hard to explain. It's like I could just snap my fingers or something and I'd wake up from this dream. It's like I'm going to wake up and you'll all disappear."

"Pretty strange, Bub."

"I mean, what if I'm not so ordinary after all? What if I'm dreaming all this? What if I'm really creating everything? How would I know it?"

"Well, I got news for you, Bub, I'm here, and I'm real. I can tell you that."

"But if I'm dreaming you, then part of my dream would be you telling me that you're real. Everything could be happening like that, couldn't it?"

"No, Bub. I see you sitting there, and believe me, you're not dreaming me. You can't snap your fingers and make me disappear."

100

"Well, I'm sure you're right. But sometimes I feel that way, that's all."

"All right, why don't you go ahead try it then?"

"Try it?"

"Yeah, go ahead and snap your fingers, and let's see what happens."

"Right now?"

"Sure, just go ahead and snap your fingers."

"You sure?"

"Sure I'm sure. Just do it. Snap your fingers."

"Okay."

Snap.

# TRAIN NUMBER FOUR

Speeding along so free—
just me and train number four.
I drove her gently all night
'til light of day felt her might
and dwelt within her beauty—
the duty of the sun.
I had fun
driving the morning run.
All happy, bright and sunny—
wasn't that a funny situation?
Blue with illusion waste,
formed with the haste of life,
aged in time
like vintage wine.
Forever mine!
All the fine members of train number four
will go
as soon as the rain nears.
Still no
sane tears will take their place.
Anything—
or the race would surely be lost.

Surely the cost would not be worth it
if the day were empty and blue,
if the day were here without you.

# THE DOSTRASIS OF GAN

Once upon a time, there was Gan.

And all the belated actors ran away. People were very confused and marooned in those days.

So, the big man (some say he was extremely intelligent) said to his various servants and their families that this can't be, can it? What would the mothers of nature do if this situation were left like this for too long?

Of all the worlds that the big man had ever seen, none—repeat: none at all—had ever been so depressed and lonely with so many people. It was a land of high-gloss paint and easy-coffee serenades. But all that was about to change. The big man could feel the winds of upheaval blowing in from the sea.

That very afternoon, there was scheduled a grand march of the local priests, just as soon as they stopped by the church and picked up their gowns and frowns and pre-packaged feasts. What a monumental day was planned! Even the huge castle, where lived the big man, was to be attended to.

Surveying the scene, the big man now felt, more than ever, that he should not have put his castle right at the end of the public mall, where all the public attenders could easily attend to it. Little did any anxious sod know that belated actors, related factors and the big man would all soon meet. Disaster seemed imminent, unless, of course, the big man could get his thoughts together quicker than anyone would expect. You should never be surprised at anything when you are living in a land of half-lit candles.

Time was behaving orderly as the millions and millions of distinct but gray creatures began their greasy march up the mall toward the frightfully calendar-like castle where lived the big man. It was an unforgettable sight. No eyes blinked.

The marchers were clearly not the heroes of Gan. Nor were they comrades of the big man. They were, however, determined to confront the excruciating turmoil they carried within them. And, as we all know, there is nothing more worthy of notice than raw, unrestrained motivation on the move.

Somehow, either by himself or with the help of his distant dreams, the big man made his wish (which he wished) come true. The transformation occurred in plain view. Everyone could see it—everyone, that is, who could see the big man in the first place.

The big man always did like islands. He found the concept of an isolated splotch of land fascinating and inviting. So, what better place for his castle than on a lush, green island in the middle of the ocean. He walked with eager mind out of his castle onto the white-sand beach. From there he followed an old trail deep into the forest, a forest thick with trees and other things that forests are known to have.

He wandered around that forest for hours. At last, he came to rest on a large stump next to a mighty pine. He took a deep breath and let the air out slowly.

You might have thought, if you hadn't known him, that the big man was lost. But he knew where he was.

He knew exactly where he was.

He wished he had packed a lunch, though.

# THIS CHILD

There's no one in the church tonight.
There's no one at your home.
I've been all around this half-baked town,
And still I am alone.
If I had a little more sense,
Do you think I'd be out here?
I'd be back in my easy chair
With my favorite brand of beer.

Oh, won't you please help me?
Help me with my fears.
If I had a little more trust than you,
Do you think I'd need these tears?
Come on, give me comfort.
Please stay with me a while.
If I can just get through this time,
I'll show you I can smile.

Now back in the days of olden,
When the people stood so tall,
I wondered where I'd fit in this
When I had learned it all.

Well, somehow we all got older,
The papers and the pens and like that.
And now I stand here looking 'round
And wondering where I'm at.

Oh, won't you please help me?
Help me with my pain.
If I had a little more faith than you,
Do you think I'd be insane?
Come on, give me comfort.
Please stay with me for now.
If I can just get through this time,
I'll pay you back somehow.

I look back on it fondly,
The days that were spent in play.
If somebody asked me what become of them,
I just don't know what I'd say.
When I get off of this trolley,
I'm gonna pick up a hot dog and bun,
And make it on out to the baseball park,
And try and have some fun.

Oh, won't you please help me?
Help me with my greed.
If I had a little more love than you,
Do you think I'd have this need?
Come on, give me comfort.
Please stay with me all night.
If I can just get through this time,
I'm sure I'll be all right.

Well, I'm asking you this one last favor.
Come teach me something to say.
And take me all around this great big world
And have me back home in a day.
And if you don't think it's worth the risk,
Then you've forgotten what you've done.
A real soft voice told me long ago
That you and I are one.

Oh, won't you please help me!
Help me with my grief.
If I had a little more hope than you,
Do you think I'd seek relief?
Come on, give me comfort!
Please stay with me for good.
If I can just get through this time,
I'll be just like I should.

Albert Einstein was a simple man.
He hardly ever combed his hair.
He told us that the past and the future
Were neither here nor there.
When I finally remember who I am,
And the world that I've lost sight of,
Then all the stars in the universe
Will come and join this child in love.

# LOOKING FOR JIMMY

Speckers wants to glare on me. I told him that the Blue Aaron would never allow such a thing. Sporn on you Speckers! I can't even remember how long it's been since I gave sporn, probably not since that old lady in the Dratley house. I can still see her standing at the side of the lake, rounding up all the loons she tried to keep in her back yard. One by one, they all escaped, never to be seen again. Oh, well. Maybe that didn't happen anyway.

Anyway, what do I have to complain about?

Oh, in case you're wondering, Jason's down at the carnival right now. But when he comes back, I'll tell him you were here. I hope you have lots of fun on your trip. They say the sight-seeing's really great up there.

Oh, oh! I think Jimmy's disappeared again, so I need to go look for him. He just started this disappearing act about a week ago, and he's been on my nerves ever since. I swear, it's worse than when we had the flood.

I hope he's not out back. It's never been solidified back there. They say the whole region is not really where it seems to be. I'm sure that's where he went, though. He loves it back there. I shouldn't even go back there myself, but I've just got to find my Jimmy. You want to come along while I look? Okay, let's go.

Wow! Aren't these trees outrageous?

Pretty cool how the dew glistens, huh?

Check out that pond. See the willows on the far side?

Hey, who's that coming down the trail over there to the right? This is weird. Who could that be? Whoa, it looks like... No! It can't be. Yes! It is. It's Speckers! And he's carrying a loon.

"Hi, Speckers."

"Hi."

"Want to come with us?"

"No, thanks. I don't know where you're going."

"We're headed into the woods. You don't happen to know where Jimmy is, do you?"

"No. Why?"

"Because I need to find him. He's disappeared again."

"So? Let him go."

"I can't do that! I have to find him."

"Well, then, why don't you come along with me. I'm headed to the carnival. Maybe he's there."

"That does make sense."

"But I don't want your friend coming with us."

"Why not?"

"Isn't that obvious? Do you think I want to be seen with someone like that? Besides, those type of people don't belong here in the first place."

"Yeah, I guess you're right."

"So, say good-bye and come along."

"All right."

Good-bye. You do understand, don't you?

# WOMAN ON HIGH

Brozo held his mud to her.
She didn't ride his rays.
Her face was made with days of joys
And boys who smoothed her skin.
To win, she flashed her smiles.
Styles built her platform—high above the crowds.
Clouds are for thunder.
Time is for passing.
Dirt's for the poor.
She's for then—when names were under the floor.

# JOE (and ours)

Brandon stayed behind with Mitch. The shells just keep on falling. "Look out, Dagg!" What a bitch!

Gordon's second file fell out at the last ditch. Now we're trapped. The third platoon's up front somewhere. No tellin' what they'll do. Maybe we'll pull through this somehow. But I doubt it. War ain't no fun, I'll tell ya.

Blame the flame. Blame the ass-sucker at the desk right now filing the Cooper Estate Report. Screw the nice panties and nice legs. Why should he have them? He's wrinkled anyway. His face is pocked and chubby, and he stinks like his crotch.

"Blow his head of, Snide!" These barbs are sharp. "Let's get the hell outa here, men!" We don't stand a chance. Damn basic was never like this.

I wish them dick-wads would stay the hell off the front lines. God, I never saw such a mess. Bodies, blood... Christ, we don't have a prayer.

Hey, wait, Flanley! Stay down here. Hey, Flanley can't possibly be floating in the air, can he? "Wipe that smile off your face, Flanley." What the hell's he doing drifting up to the sky anyway? God, I'm crackin' up!

Can't wait to get the hell outa here and drivin' my rod back home. Hottest thing in town, man. The lousy southsiders know where it's at, too. I wipe their asses all over the street with it. Shit, ain't nobody lick me. I remember the time me and Jackson took on every one of them bastards from the south side. Christ, what a day that was. Yeah. Me and Jackson had some good times in those days. Easy-ass Jackson went Navy, though. I think he's gettin' out June after next. I bet when we get back together, we do some crazier shit than we ever done. Damn cops, I'd like to kill every one of 'em. Never could pin anything on me and Jackson, though. Me and Jackson had the town by the balls, man. Bet the place ain't been the same, last two years. Momma sure was sad to see me enlist, that's for sure. Poor momma.

Christ, what's goin' on here? What's all this flesh hangin' down here?

Bootie, bootie, bootie, dum de dum.

Gimme my gun! Where'd it go? I'll blow the damn heads off every one of them damn bastards. I hate 'em. Hey, where'd this foot come from? How come I don't hear no more gunfire? Jesus! Where's Archie's men, anyway?

Wait a second! Buses can't fly! Get that bus of fags the hell out of here. And tell them to quit staring at me. I oughta kill 'em all. They deserve it.

God damn flesh gettin' in the way. It's all over. Blood, too. How come I keep falling? Hey, how come I keep falling? I know this ain't right. Who can I ask about this?

Everything's all flipped over every which way. Nothing makes no sense no more. All the know-it-alls must have gone out to lunch. It's all a mess.

Damn, ain't that a sight! Red sky flashing on and off, yellow or blue or some shit. Ha-ha! Some chick just got her ass nailed, I know it.

Some guys dig holding up brown. Some guys dig feeling gold. Brown and gold growing old for sure. I must be dreaming. But I ain't got no thoughts. Falling forever. Never hitting bottom, and never moving. Water and dirt are way above me now. No direction to go. How far above is home?

There ain't no blue-eyed momma!

Sweat and urine hit the sky. Jesus can't fly his kite. Light comes from beds with heads floating under the covers. Lovers have rabies. Babies are crying, and their tears are moving Mount Everest. Everyone's grabbing what they can. It's such a major pain.

I am pure with yellow mucus. Bad? Sad or glad? Day is night. Right is wrong. I belong nowhere. I am zero.

Fear!

I fear. I can't stop shaking. End to all. Loud! Crashing, bashing, speeding, flashing! All is nothing.

Thick and shapeless, flying without moving. Up, down, round and round. Faster and faster. No ground, no sound. No sight. Everything. Everywhere. Mother. Great-grandfather. Old beard. Jews and dirty windows. Windmills. Wishbones. Wood fences. Cows. First Federal Trust Bank. Ninth and Main. Dual exhaust. Coloring books. Harry the Hippo. Lightning!

Flash! Flash!

All is none is me. Seeds swirling in blood. Dick Tracy enter, stage center. Faster without form. Faster and faster and faster and I don't know.

Flash!

A room.

One single room.

A simple room without clutter.

There I stand, alone in the hall, looking into the room through one of the glass walls. I take a minute or two to focus on the details of the room.

The room is, I would say, about ten feet wide and about twenty feet long. All the walls are glass. The floor and ceiling are shiny silver. The room contains six machines lined up in a row lengthwise down the middle of the room. Each machine has a label at its base, and each label says "Feeding Unit."

Each of the feeding units looks somewhat like a redesigned barber chair. My eyes scan one of the units. The unit is about two feet in diameter at the base and stands about four feet tall. It has four steel prongs that came up from the base and support a tiny piece of flesh-colored material directly above the unit. The flesh-like material is labeled "exis." I estimate the size of the exis to be about a half inch across. There are what look like hundreds of tiny wires attached to the exis. The wires flow into a cable that goes into the floor. All six units look identical in every detail. The entire setup appears very shiny, obviously sanitary.

I stand outside the glass, looking into the room.

Several minutes pass.

Suddenly, a man enters the room from the other end. He is a tall man and a picture of cleanliness. He is wearing white clothes and white rubber gloves. We glance at each other through the glass. He sees me, but doesn't seem to mind that I am there observing. He quickly goes about his business.

He walks directly to the fourth unit down from my end and proceeds to disconnect the tiny wires from the exis. Since there are many wires, it takes some time for him to do this. I watch intently. When all the wires are unhooked, he removes the exis from the grip of the securing steel prongs. He very gently places the exis in a white cloth. He wraps it carefully and then leaves the room through the same door from which he entered. I surmise that there are now only five feeding units operative in the room.

I hear the man's footsteps echoing in the hall. I can tell he is headed around the outside of the room to the hallway where I am. As he comes around the corner, he is carrying the wrapped cloth in both hands. He walks up and stops next to me.

"Howdy," he says.

"Hello," I reply.

We both stand there silently for a moment.

"Quite a setup," he asserts.

"Sure is." I mean it, too.

"Yeah," he says, taking a breath, "we need to get another one going on unit number four, though. Now that this one's run through."

We both turn and stare into the room. Without uttering a word, we stand and watch the silent operation of the machines.

After a minute or so, he turns back to me. "Isn't it amazing?"

I nod in agreement.

"Just think," he says, "each one is a separate life being run through, every detail. There are feed-ins for touch, sight, smell, taste, hearing as well as every known emotion. Everything that is needed to program an entire life is there. They thought of everything."

"Incredible." I am truly amazed.

"And what's even more impressive is that the whole operation is perfectly coordinated. The coordination is the thing that makes it work."

"It's hard to imagine that it really does work," I offer.

"Oh, it does. No doubt about that."

"I guess it must."

"Think of it this way," he explains. "Suppose you were watching a movie at a theater, and you were sitting so close to the screen that you couldn't see off the edges. Then that movie would be all you would know visually, right?"

"Uhh... I guess so. Sure."

"Well, it's like that. Each exis is being shown an entire life, as if it were seeing everything through its own eyes. And the whole thing has to be coordinated with all the other feed-ins. Get it? The coordination is the key."

I ponder the man's words for a moment. "What do you mean by coordination?" I ask.

"Well, for example, if we send in through the sight feed-ins that your view is changing from the ground to the sky, then we also need to feed in the sensation of moving your head upward. This has to happen at exactly the same time. Or let's say we feed in the sensation of extending your arm, then simultaneously, we must also feed in a perfectly coordinated visual image of you seeing your arm being extended. You follow what I'm saying?"

"I think so."

"It's even more confusing with the thought processes. With thoughts, so many different things are all interrelated and interacting at the same time. You should see some of the cognition diagrams the programmers study to figure this stuff out. You wouldn't believe how complex

**118**

everything is. And on top of that, we need to constantly accompany actions and emotions with feed-ins of autonomy. Feelings of self-awareness are absolutely essential, so that it seems to the recipient that they are actually making decisions."

The man pauses briefly to admire the room again. "It's all very mind-boggling," he continues. "It took me almost six years just to understand the principles behind the operation of the Dukemaster board."

I figure that thing must be really complicated. "Does any of it every have equipment trouble?" I ask.

"I've never known a case."

"I am really impressed."

We both gaze into the room, transfixed.

Then the man glances at his watch.

"Well, hey," he says, "I've gotta run. We got a meeting at four, so I better go. It was nice talking to you."

"Okay, so long."

He turns to leave. Then stops. "Oh, one more thing," he says, "If you're going to stick around here much longer, keep an eye open for that nut in the red sweater."

"Who?" I'm not sure I heard him correctly.

"Oh, some crazy guy in a red sweater keeps running up and down the halls in here muttering stupid things to himself. We've been trying to round him up for about two hours now."

"Is he dangerous? Do I need to worry?"

"Naw, I don't think so. At least he doesn't appear to be. Nothing to worry about. He just keeps saying things that don't make any sense, that's all."

"Like what does he say?" I ask

"Oh, just nonsense, that's all."

**119**

"Like what?"

"Oh, nothing worth repeating." The man chuckles.

"I'm curious. Like what does he say?"

"Well, he keeps shouting some nonsense about a higher level. He keeps saying there is another level after this one. He keeps yelling, 'You wouldn't know, you wouldn't know.' Whatever the heck that means. He keeps saying, 'Where does it end, where does it end?' Dumb stuff like that."

I think to myself, Who can I ask about this?

"Quite honestly," he continues, "I have no idea what the guy is talking about."

The man pauses, looks at the floor, and then looks at me again. "But, hey, don't you worry about him. Look, if he shows up, just go throw that big switch on the wall over there, okay?"

I see the switch. "Okay."

"That will bring the guard."

The man glances at his watch again. "Well, I absolutely need to go now. I'm late. I'll see you later. Bye."

"Bye."

The man hurries away carrying the white cloth. I watch as he rounds a far corner and disappears from sight.

I decide to stay and watch the operation of the room a little while longer, until I think of something else to do.

The man in the red sweater hasn't come by yet.

# A START

A start can be an end,
And a friend may be a stone,
When you're grown enough to see.

# THE MAGIC MIRROR

Spaulding James was a dirty man. His skin hadn't been washed in days, his clothes in weeks. Actually, he was just like any other common person in the far away land of Bester.

The residents of Bester were divided into two classes. The common people made up more than ninety-nine percent of the population. The kings comprised the remaining fraction of a percent. The common people had no possessions and were forced to work all day in factories. The kings lived luxuriously and never labored. The kings were able to suppress the common people by means of a well-armed Kings Army.

One day, a king's servant presented the kings with a gift. The servant had spent many weeks creating this strange gift: a magic mirror.

This particular mirror did not reflect light like an ordinary mirror. No. Instead, it displayed whatever images were held subconsciously by the person standing in front of it. It exposed the person's deepest thoughts and desires, revealing them for all to see. Nothing could be kept secret from the magic mirror. No one, no matter how hard he or she tried, could prevent the mirror from revealing his or her innermost feelings.

For the mirror to work, the subject needed to stand directly in front of the glass and stare into it. Sometimes, a few minutes were required before the images would appear, but they always would. And no one, not even the subject in front of the mirror, could determine beforehand exactly what images would be shown. The mirror was full of surprises—and loads of fun.

The kings enjoyed their gift immensely. Whenever they held a party, the magic mirror was sure to be the center of attention. They would place one king in front of the mirror, and all the other kings and queens would stand to the side and observe the show. Watching the mirror was great entertainment for all.

More often than not, the shows consisted of strange paradises. Sometimes a king would visualize himself in a land of naked women feeding him delicious foods and throwing orgies in his honor. Sometimes a king would picture a land in which money grew on trees and the common people went out every day to harvest it for the kings. Sometimes one of the kings would visualize himself whipping huge numbers of common people and forcing them to endure terrible torture. The shows varied according to the personal tastes and idiosyncrasies of the particular king standing in front of it.

Every once in a while, the mirror would lead an to altercation among the kings. If one of the kings happened to visualize himself making love to another king's woman, tempers would flare. Usually, however, these disagreements were not serious, since the kings agreed that the display in the mirror was only an image and not reality. The kings also realized that, although the images may be based on some inner longing, those images were not anything the subject would likely ever act on, nor were the images anything the subject could control.

Things got really interesting when the kings started placing their queens in front of the mirror. Many secret longings were revealed this way. One king discovered that his queen wanted to have another child but had never told him so. Another king learned that his queen had seduced his brother a few years back. That revelation led to a duel. Usually, when a queen was the subject, the mirror showed scenes that were more sensual and erotic than when a king was the subject. The kings enjoyed these shows tremendously.

The magic mirror proved to be magnificent entertainment for many months. No other item in the kingdom was so much fun.

As time went on, however, the kings grew tired of their new toy. They noticed that many of the shows were starting to repeat. Some of the shows had been displayed a dozen times or more. The kings began to grumble. Some of the kings complained that all possible shows had already been shown.

It got to a point where, as soon as the mirror would start to display a scene, the kings would groan in unison. They immediately recognized the show, and they already knew what was going to happen. They had definitely become bored with their magic mirror. Everyone was eager for a new and different show.

Late one evening, after a particularly dull party, one of the kings spoke up. "Hey," he said, "I have an idea. The problem is that we all know each other so well. We always pick one of our group of kings or queens to stand in front of the mirror. What we need is someone different, someone

we don't know, someone not within our immediate circle."
The king had everyone's attention. "May I suggest," he
went on, "just for a laugh, that we send a squad of the
Kings Army out onto the street to select at random one
of the common people. We'll place him in front of the
mirror to see what foolery his vision yields."

The idea was an immediate hit. Everyone realized what
fantastic fun this could be.

One of the older kings spoke up saying, "Surely, a common person's images would be greatly different from any
of ours, since the mind of a common person is vastly infe-
rior and uncultured compared to that of we learned kings.
Such an exercise should prove greatly amusing. I say, let's
do it!"

All the kings stood and cheered.

"He'll probably have a world with common people rul-
ing over kings," shouted one king.

"He may wish to make love to all our fair queens,"
yelled another king.

"Things he would never tell us to our faces will be
shown in the mirror, and he won't even be able to control
it," shouted another.

Everyone in the room laughed and laughed.

Agreement was unanimous.

Spaulding James was casually walking down the street
when he was taken. The soldiers seized him and carried
him off without a word of explanation. It's hard to say
why they selected Spaulding from the crowded avenue.
Maybe they picked him because he had that simple look
of humility. The kings despised that look. Maybe they
chose him because of his small build. Maybe he really
was selected at random. We'll never know.

125

The party was especially lively that night. The kings decided to make the magic mirror the last event of the evening. Until then, Spaulding lay face up in the middle of the floor, naked—his hands and feet chained. The party took place all around him, as the kings and queens ate, drank and frolicked. The festivities were loud and wild.

The party-goers made fun of Spaulding lying on the floor. From time to time, a king would walk by and poke him or kick him. Sometimes, a king or queen would spit on him and others would laugh. One king even set fire to his hair and put it out with wine. Through it all, Spaulding never spoke a word. He knew better than to question.

At last, the main event of the evening was at hand. All the drunken kings and queens gathered around the magic mirror. Spaulding James was carried over and placed upright in front of the mirror. The kings decided not to give Spaulding any explanation of what was to happen, so that he, too, would be surprised as he stared into the glass. They hoped the common man would not know that he was responsible for the nature of the show. With his hands and feet chained, Spaulding James stood directly in front of the mirror.

A hush fell over the room. Spaulding looked directly into the mirror. Everyone watched.

At first, the mirror remained blank. It stayed that way for an unusually long time, what seemed like several minutes. Some of the kings began growing impatient, wondering if perhaps something was wrong. Maybe a common man was so ignorant that nothing of substance was in his subconscious mind. Maybe the mirror would not work at all with someone so unworthy. The crowd began rustling.

Then... something started happening. In the center of the mirror, there appeared a tiny dot of white light. Slowly, the light started to grow.

As the light became larger, it became clearer. At the same time, the light began pulsating, brighter and weaker. And then, it started changing colors.

The kings and queens watched quietly.

The light started alternating colors at a rapid pace. It was changing hue so quickly you could never, at any one instant, discern its precise color. Then the light started flashing. Seconds later, the light was flashing brightly.

Around the edges of the display, little sparkling crystals began to form. They grew sharper and more distinct. Then, suddenly, they spread across the entire mirror, as though a film of water were running down the face of the glass.

A second later, the bright flashing stopped. The mirror was then covered with thousands of sparkling crystals.

The crystals began to move. They began circling around and around, faster and faster. Then, in a dazzling display of wonder, the crystals melted into one another, unfolding a beautiful bright rainbow of radiant colors. The mirror was soon filled with a circular swirling stream of dazzling light, marbled with an infinity of distinct, glowing colors.

The colors continued swirling faster and faster.

And then, from out of nowhere, came hundreds of tiny angels flapping their wings and flying around in the stream of colors. Suddenly, the entire mirror began flashing again.

The colors continued to swirl, faster and faster. The little angels began kissing one another randomly. The colors started mixing faster, continually shifting. All over the mirror, angels were dancing and hugging one another, constantly darting about changing partners. If you looked carefully, you could see smiles on their tiny faces.

The pace quickened.

And the brightness grew.

The scene was impossible to describe—colors flashing, crystals swirling—clockwise and counterclockwise, up and down, in and out. Everything was moving and flashing. The mirror was glowing and pulsating so brightly that the human eye could scarcely bear to look at it. It was a scene of blinding brilliance.

The kings watched the show in a state of bewilderment. Gradually, they became irritated. They began to fidget and murmur among themselves, trying to figure out what might be the meaning of this gaudy display. They did not like it one little bit.

Finally, one of the kings stepped forward. "He mocks us!" he shouted angrily.

A roar of agreement rose from the crowd.

"I've had enough of this. How about all of you?" he yelled.

The crowd threw their fists in air as they shouted agreement.

The king who spoke ran to the fireplace mantle across the room. Without delay, he drew a sword and rushed back to Spaulding. He pulled back his arm and placed the point of the sword at Spaulding's side, prepared to thrust the blade through Spaulding's naked body.

"Kill! Kill! Kill!" the crowd chanted in unison.

"Shall I?" the king yelled.

"Kill! Kill! Kill!" continued the chant.

"I will. I will," yelled the king.

"Kill! Kill! Kill!" The chant was deafening.

Just then, Spaulding James, with his hands and feet chained, turned from the mirror and faced the king who was holding the sword. Spaulding stared gently into the eyes of the king, just as he had been staring into the mirror.

And all the world folded into crystal flashing.

Dusk into mildness without worry

# CAZON AND STENLEY

Cazon and Stenley were the best of friends. They grew up on the same mountaintop and shared their youthful years together.

"Oh, my God!" Stenley exclaimed one day as he stood before the looking glass. "It happened!"

"But it happens to everyone," Cazon reminded him. "And so we, too, must enter this stage of life they call early manhood."

Being the adventurous sort that they were, Cazon and Stenley decided they must set out to reap whatever fruits the planet had to offer. They agreed to go their separate ways.

With jolly speed, Cazon and Stenley each built a sled of their own and assembled a team of dogs.

The day finally arrived, the day they had agreed upon to bid farewell to one another. The two friends mounted their sleds.

"Let us commence our journeys at the exact same instant," Cazon declared.

With that, they each gave a snap of their whip.

But only one team of dogs began running.

Cazon was off like a flash and quickly out of sight. But Stenley did not move. His dogs would not budge.

Years passed.

Cazon traveled the world. He enjoyed the cultures of many lands. He made many deep and lasting friendships. He enjoyed many riches—and many women. He sat with many learned teachers. He gained much knowledge and wisdom. He reveled in the bounty of all creation—spreading love wherever he stopped. But always, he moved on, trying to cover the entire world, leaving no land without his visit.

Meanwhile, Stenley sat mounted on his sled, his dogs refusing to move. Day after day, he tried in vain to begin his travels. Finally, he gave up.

Many more years passed.

Long, long years.

Both men grew old.

One day, Stenley was outside gathering water, when he saw a figure upon the horizon heading his way. When the man was close enough to see, he recognized his old friend Cazon.

"Cazon!" he screamed with joy. "I had given up hope of ever seeing you again. How is it that you are here?"

"Dear Stenley," Cazon replied, "I have traveled to all points of the world. I have seen much. My life has been full and prosperous, successful by all standards. And now, my travels have carried me a complete circle around the globe. At last, I have returned to the starting point. Once again, I..."

Cazon stopped suddenly and looked down at Stenley. "But you, dear Stenley! How is it that you are here? Did you not travel the world also?"

"Oh, Cazon," Stenley said sadly. "I fear I have missed much—for I have remained here all the while. Now we are both old and feeble, and you have so much that you have accomplished. You have so many wonderful memories. You have such a vast store of contentment. And I am but a poor fool who has nothing, nothing more than that which I had so many years ago when last we stood together on this very spot."

"Dear Stenley, your words are so sad." Cazon's voice trailed off.

Just then, something remarkable caught their attention. Another figure was approaching from the horizon.

Stenley spoke. "In the distance, I see someone heading our way. This is strange, indeed. Many years I have remained here, and never has anyone, until this day, entered my sight. How very peculiar. I wonder who this wandering soul might be."

As soon as the mysterious man was within range, he drew back his bow and let his arrow fly. The arrow went straight into Cazon's heart. Then the man shot a second arrow, which made its way to Stenley.

Perhaps the man was a gentleman, though. Before he moved on, he dug a proper grave for the two of them and marked it well. Then, the wandering archer walked away whistling.

Now, it so happens that the location where these events transpired is on a mountaintop high above the clouds. And every day, the sun shines brightly on that very spot where Cazon and Stenley lie side by side.

# ABOUT THE AUTHOR

Victor Boc has been...

- A top-rated radio personality, who has hosted radio programs nationally, as well as in major cities across the country. He was awarded a place among "The Most Important Talk Show Hosts in America."

- A world-class professional poker player, who has won numerous tournaments and competed in the World Series of Poker.

- A best-selling author, whose book, "How to Solve All Your Money Problems Forever," sold more than 200,000 copies worldwide.

- A popular nightclub deejay and entertainer.

- A highly-respected business consultant.

Victor has also ridden a motorcycle across country, climbed Telescope Peak, and slept with a bear.

These days, Victor consults businesses, produces teen dances, designs websites—and plays poker. Living in the beautiful state of Oregon, he devotes a great deal of time to hiking and romping outdoors. He plays baseball with his son—and lets their pet ferret run free around the house.

## VICTOR'S HUMBLE REQUEST

I love customer reviews on Amazon.com! So, I humbly request that you write me one. Please?

Write your review here:
**justlivingandreproducing.com/ab**

This link will send you to Amazon.com. Scroll down the Amazon page until you see the "Customer Reviews" section, and click the button to write a review. There you can express your thoughts, whatever they are.

If you write a review, send me an email message (at victorboc@outlook.com) and tell me which review is yours. I'd like to say thank you.

---

## ALSO BY VICTOR BOC

*How to Solve All Your Money Problems Forever*
*Creating a Positive Flow of Money Into your Life*
flowofmoney.com/ab
flowofomoney.com

*The Five Greatest Secrets of Poker and Life*
fivegreatestsecrets.com/ab
fivegreatestsecrets.com

*Money Talks*

*Beyond Your Wildest Dreams*

*Georgia Bear Can't Dance*

*"Even when you don't hear my thoughts,
I am still thinking them."*

a West Coast Bee

JUST LIVING AND REPRODUCING
— A Collection of Stories and Such —
Victor Boc
2013

www.ingramcontent.com/pod-product-compliance
Lightning Source LLC
Chambersburg PA
CBHW030625130626
46552CB00002B/708